I0556842

NORTH POLE UNLIMITED COLLECTION 2

NICK & EVE, RUDY & KRIS

ELLE RUSH

SBD ENTERTAINMENT

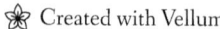

NICK AND EVE

A North Pole Unlimited Romance
By
Elle Rush

BLURB

Nick's plan: dodge his grandmother's matchmaking attempts by claiming Eve is his date for Christmas. He probably should have asked Eve first.

Although Nick Klassen is grateful when Eve rides to his rescue after he breaks down outside of December, Manitoba, he can't run fast enough when his meddling grandmother tries to set him up with the pretty tow-truck driver. Then he gets an idea.

Between juggling extra hours at work and a never-ending Christmas to-do list, Eve LeBlanc doesn't have time for a new man in her life. But ever since she picked Nick up on the side of the road, she's been running into him everywhere.

His deception started innocently enough but when his grandmother invites his fake girlfriend to the family's Christmas dinner, Nick realizes that he must come clean. Once Eve learns what he's been doing, he'll need Santa's help to turn their pretend relationship into the real thing.

1. NICK

"OH, THE WEATHER OUTSIDE IS—" Nick Klassen jabbed the power button to the radio to silence the perky voice coming through the truck's speakers. He knew exactly what the weather was like. The bright sun blazing off the snow-covered fields and the clear skies made it look like a nice, warm day, but the weather station and his cold nose told him the air was more frigid than normal in the month before Christmas.

The view was nice enough that he wouldn't have minded the cold if his heater worked, but it, like the engine, had died. Nick tugged his toque lower on his head, pulled up the cuffs of his mittens, and settled in to wait for help to arrive.

It didn't take long. He spotted the tow truck in his rear-view mirror. When it got closer, he turned in his seat to stare directly out the back window to ensure he wasn't hallucinating.

The bar of yellow caution lights and twin spotlights on the roof were festooned with red and gold garland. A wreath the width of his forearm was wired to the front grill. He couldn't see into the cab well enough to give a description of the driver, but he was certain he saw a plush red hat with a white brim and pompom.

He was being rescued by Santa Claus. He'd never live this down at the office.

The tow truck pulled to a stop in front of his dead classic. When the driver's door opened, Nick was surprised to see a woman half as tall as her vehicle hop out. She checked for traffic before she approached his window. "Hi. Are you Nick?"

She had the same voice as the caroller on the radio, but he liked this one's cheerful nature. "You bet. Wow, you're fast." He'd called for service ten minutes ago. It had felt like an hour, but the time on his phone said differently. She must have left the second she got his request. "I appreciate it."

"No problem. I'm Eve. Do you know what went wrong with your awesome truck?" she asked.

It was an awesome truck; he was happy she recognized the fact. Driving the heavy beast from the 1940s was like driving a tank, but Nick loved the classic lines. The flawless red paint job and gleaming chrome drew looks, too. He got comments every time he drove her into the city. Unfortunately, looks only got him so far; the maintenance was killing him. "I know the battery works. It's new. It must be the engine."

"I could have helped you with the battery," she said. "For anything else, I can hook you up for a tow and take you back to December."

"I'll take the tow, but can I ask for a favour? I was on the way to pick up my grandmother and take her to the doctor. Her house is about five kilometres from here. Can you drive me there instead? She has a car I can use, and we can still make her appointment."

Eve considered his request for a moment. "If you're comfortable leaving me your keys, we can do that. I'll drop you off, then come back for your truck. Where do you want it to go? Webster's Garage?"

It was the only garage in December. Happily, it was the also the best one in the southern part of Manitoba when it came to classic trucks. "Webster's is fine."

"Get into my truck and warm up. I'll be there shortly."

Nick almost offered to help, but she was the professional, and he was cold. In the minute it took for his fingers to thaw as he held them over the blasting heat, Eve set reflective triangles around his vehicle. "Where are we going?" she asked as she jumped into the driver's seat and held her hands over the vents on her side.

The directions were simple—three kilometres down the highway and a left turn, which lead straight to his mother's family homestead. They'd long ago sold the farmland, but they'd kept the house and a few hectares around it. It was too much for one person, but his grandmother refused to leave. Nick and his cousins had encouraged her to move into town, especially if her medical condition kept her from driving permanently, but Adelaide was resisting. The appointment that afternoon would provide the final verdict on her licence.

Eve rolled to a stop in the driveway. "This is impressive." Strings of Christmas lights framed the two-storey house and circled the spruce tree in the front yard. Plastic candy canes stuck in the snowbanks lined the sidewalk, and a pinecone-studded wreath, twice the size of the one on the tow-truck's grill, hung from the screen door.

"You should see the inside. Can you wait till I'm certain her car will start? She hasn't run it in a couple weeks," Nick said.

His grandmother must have been watching from the window, because the front door opened before they hit the first step. "Come in, it's freezing out here," she said.

The entranceway and the adjacent living room were fully Christmas-bombed, from the reindeer-shaped sofa cushions to the double-decker, white candy bowl stand, which had a Frosty face and top hat stuck to the top of the wire frame. Nick held back a snicker as Eve spun in a three-sixty and breathed a quiet, "Whoa."

"You're not kidding," he whispered back.

"I'm Adelaide Klassen. Who might you be?" his gran asked. She was dressed for her appointment. After a lifetime of seeing her in business suits at the office, it was always a shock to Nick's system to see his grey-haired grandmother in jeans and a plaid flannel shirt.

Eve gave Adelaide's hand a hearty shake. "Eve LeBlanc, tow truck driver."

A thoughtful look crossed Adelaide's face. "LeBlanc. Are you Paul's daughter?"

Eve winced. "I'm Helen Gauthier's daughter."

Adelaide's look turned confused. "I could have sworn Paul said his daughter drove a tow truck. Anyway, it's lovely to meet you. Are you a special friend of Nick's?"

Nick sighed. She was starting, and they'd only been in the house for thirty seconds. "No, Gran, she's not my girlfriend."

"I just picked him up on the side of the road. I must say he is the cutest stray I've come across in a while," Eve added with a smile.

"Don't encourage her!" But it was flattering to know

Eve thought he was cute. "Gran, can I have your keys? We'll have to take your car, since Eve is taking my truck to the shop."

Adelaide pointed to a key hook behind the door. "Be sure to take it to Webster's Garage. Their mechanics have been fixing the old girl since my husband used to own it."

"I will," Eve promised.

That was sweet of her, going along like she was following his grandmother's suggestion and he and she hadn't already come to that decision.

"Nick, you're early. Do we all have some time for cocoa?" Adelaide raised her hand, fending off his protest before he could voice it. "My doctor okayed it. It's made from skim milk and artificial sweetener, but it's better than nothing. Barely."

"I really need to be going. I have to hook up Nick's truck, and every minute without a call is a break these days," Eve said. She took off her red hat and pushed blonde bangs off her forehead. "Thank you, though."

"I have chocolate caramel shortbread cookies, too."

Eve hesitated before shaking her head. "Tempting, but I can't."

"The least we can do is give you a snack for the road. After all, you didn't have to drive Nick to my place. You could have insisted he go back to town with his truck. Let me get some for you." The wily senior disappeared around the corner, and Nick heard a drawer open.

"Take them," he whispered. "Her shortbread is legendary."

"I never turn down shortbread. Don't you have a car to start?" Eve asked.

He did—a monster SUV made for Manitoba winter driving with an engine that put his to shame, but it had sat in a garage for an extended period. He hoped it wouldn't have any problem turning over.

It didn't.

He left it running and returned to the house. Eve was putting a bag of cookies into her coat pocket. "All good?" she asked.

"No problem." He handed her his truck keys. "Tell Gordon I'll stop by later this afternoon."

"Will do. Why don't you give me your number, and I'll text you when I drop it off?"

"That would be great." Even if the garage didn't have time to look at it today, he'd know it was safe on the premises. Nick quickly programmed his number into the proffered cell phone, and Eve immediately sent him a text to ensure he got it.

"We have a plan. Thanks for the cookies, Mrs. Klassen." She slipped her hat onto her head, adjusting the pompom so it hung just above her right ear. "Merry Christmas."

And as suddenly as she'd arrived in his life, Eve was gone. The last thing he saw before she pulled out of the yard was her setting the bag of cookies on the dashboard and taking one out.

His grandma poked him in the shoulder with a bony finger he felt through his coat. "What was wrong with that one? You aren't getting any younger, you know."

He'd heard that refrain often since his grandmother's retirement. There was nothing wrong with Eve. She was pretty, and kind, and strong, and smart enough to be a successful independent contractor in a primarily male business. He respected all of that, but none of it mattered when he'd scheduled himself to work overtime tonight in order to be able to drive Adelaide to the doctor. He simply didn't have time to date. "She has poor judgment."

"That girl?"

"She picks strange men up on the side of the road," Nick said.

"She picked *you* up."

"Aren't you the one who is always saying I'm the strangest boy you know?" he countered.

She huffed and puffed but, in the end, she laughed like he knew she would. "Get in the car."

2. EVE

EVE LAY her mittens on the radiator by the front door, hoping they'd dry out in her brief interlude at home. All she wanted was to crawl under an afghan on her sofa, watch the cooking show she'd recorded the night before, and doze until it was time to go to bed. She'd had midnight call-outs for the last three days.

But she couldn't. She'd made plans.

Her phone beeped with an incoming text. "*Still up for an Operation Retriever update?*" her BFF Amanda asked.

"*Yes, see you at PP at 7,*" Eve replied.

Operation Retriever was the only thing that could motivate her to move. It had been running for three months, and the team members had decided to let it continue till the end of the year. Each meeting was more depressing as they limped along, running out of hope and time.

In a small town like December, Madison Hill and her constant canine companion were greeted by name everywhere the little girl went in her wheelchair. Business owners didn't hesitate to allow the support dog into their stores whenever the spunky cancer fighter came for a shop or a visit. Sadly, Madison's golden retriever, Bucky, had gone missing at the start of the school year after he ran away from the kennel where they'd boarded him while she underwent a multi-day treatment in Winnipeg.

Nobody knew if the dog had run away or had been stolen, but Madison insisted Bucky would come home someday. Despite the feel-good ending of *Homeward Bound*, which Madison referred to often, Eve didn't believe a runaway dog could survive four months on its own in such harsh conditions. She was certain Bucky had to be long gone by now. But for a sick little girl, they continued to look. Tonight would be a progress meeting. At least it would be a short one.

One particular icon on her phone screen continued to blink at her. It had been flashing since lunch, but Eve had done her best to ignore it. It was time to rip off the bandage.

She recognized the number, so the voice and the message weren't a surprise. "Sweetheart, I'm sorry, but I have to cancel our supper plans. You know I wouldn't do that unless—"

She spoke along with the next words. "—it was really important."

Her father continued to offer recorded platitudes. "My boss is sick and asked me to sit in on a last-minute meeting for him. I can't get out of it. I know you understand, Evie-bear. We'll get together soon."

Eve punched the little red DELETE key on the phone a little harder than necessary to rid herself of this latest parental disappointment.

She had only lied a little bit to Adelaide Klassen.

Biologically, she was Paul LeBlanc's daughter, but he had disappeared so early in her life, it was more accurate to say her mother had raised her single-handedly. Helen Gauthier was the one who'd taught her to drive and change a tire. She was the one who had gone to the school to insist they make room for Eve in the shop class when Eve had tried to enroll in it.

Eve didn't know why her father was back in town, but she'd finally listened to her mom's plea to be a good daughter and agreed to meet him. It was more than she owed him.

He'd let her down. She wasn't surprised. It was why she'd purposely double-booked herself that night. Still, Eve had given him a second chance. She wouldn't waste her time on a third.

Her phone rang while she was juggling a hot bowl straight from the microwave. She didn't get to it in time, but it rang a second time a minute later. "Hello?"

"Don't forget you have a meeting tonight," her sister said in greeting.

"I'm on my way, Emily."

"I wish I could be there, but I have a big test coming up."

"Don't worry about it. School is more important. I'll tell you everything that happens. I'll even take notes," Eve promised.

"Can you get me one of the Pumpkin Patch's Imperial cookies and drop it off with your notes? Later tonight? It'll help me study," Emily wheedled.

"Yes, I'll drop off my notes and the cookie tonight. Now go study, brat."

Her phone beeped again immediately with a text

from a new contact. *"Gordon says he'll get to my truck tomorrow. Thanks."*

After downing her leftovers, Eve tackled her outdoor gear again. She left her Santa "work" hat on its hook and grabbed her hand-knit toque instead. She wound the matching cranberry red scarf around her neck twice before pulling on her coat. After spending all day in her truck, she thought a walk would do her good despite the cold. The Pumpkin Patch was only ten blocks from her little, tiny apartment.

She was right. There was something magical about strolling in the dark when the world was covered in snow. At this time of year, all the houses were lit with coloured Christmas lights, which reflected on the snow like little fairies dancing in the yards. By the time she got to the restaurant, her face tingled from the cold, but her mind was clear of all the clutter.

There were four restaurants in town. The December Motor Inn Dining Room was attached to the largest motel in the area; it was open from noon till nine daily and had a one-page menu that hadn't changed since it opened in the seventies. Garland's Pub was attached to the dining room but had its own kitchen; it offered pub-style snacks and meals. Norma's Buns was a breakfast-and-lunch joint which closed every day at two; their offerings changed with the seasons, but Norma had been warned if her cinnamon buns ever disappeared, there would be riots.

Last was the Pumpkin Patch. Realistically, it shouldn't have survived. On paper, December didn't have the population to support a casual restaurant. When it opened a handful of years earlier, it had filled a gap the town hadn't known existed. The Pumpkin was more than a coffee shop or diner, and less than a formal dining room. It was a fun place that also served as a popular gathering spot. It didn't hurt that the owners encouraged groups using it as a meeting place during it is off-hours, from the Tuesday morning cribbage club, to the last Friday of the month book club. Eve had never attended either, but their existence meant the staff had no trouble letting Operation Retriever push a couple tables together every two weeks for meetings.

She was the last to arrive. The others had left a chair open for her. Amanda Hill, Eve's friend since high school and Madison's mother, sat on one side of the table. Short wisps of curly hair stuck out from under the toque she hadn't removed. She'd shaved her head in solidarity with her daughter after chemo stole Madison's curly locks. Bald in Manitoba during the winter was tough. Gordon Webster was beside Amanda with what might be a grease smudge in his blond-and-white beard, but Eve wasn't close enough to make a definitive determination. Next to him was George Macintyre, a recent North Pole Unlimited retiree who had time to go on a wild dog chase.

Eve sat between Joy McCall and Jilly Lewis, both current NPU employees. The redheaded Joy was peering over Jilly's shoulder, following along as Jilly demonstrated a crochet stitch.

"Am I very late?" Eve asked.

"No. We ordered you tea and gingerbread cake," Amanda said.

"The food of champions," Eve joked.

Amanda called the meeting to order once everybody was served. "In the last week, we received four tips on social media. George followed up on them, and one may be a legitimate sighting. It was near Ste. Agathe," she reported.

"I'll call all the local vets and ask them to keep their eyes peeled," Joy said.

"I'll ask my customers from around there to keep an eye out," Gordon offered.

Eve knew her part. "I'll check it out tomorrow." Amanda had to look after her daughter, Gordon had to stay at the garage, and George's knees and hips couldn't handle tramping through the bush. If the tip came in over the weekend, Jilly or Joy checked it out. However, the combination of work and short days with limited daylight meant the ladies would be stumbling around in the dark looking for a runaway dog, so Eve always got the weekday sightings.

It undoubtedly added to her work load, but she couldn't say no. There wasn't much anyone could do about the unfair assignment of duties, but they tried to make it up to her, thus the cake and tea tonight.

They knew she'd never turn down anything with caramel.

Eve missed what the next person said. She wasn't even sure who was speaking. All her attention was on the tall man with the thinning blond comb-over getting out of the booth in the corner. The man who'd said he was working late.

She looked away but not quickly enough.

"Evie-bear!"

Eve dropped her head, then pushed her chair back. If she was fast enough, what was about to happen might not turn into a scene. "Please excuse me for a minute." She didn't bother to set her napkin on the table. She wouldn't be gone that long. "Dad."

"My last-minute meeting got cancelled at the last second. I tried to call you to see if you were still available for supper, but I couldn't reach you. I came just in case you could make it."

From where she stood, she could see the remnants of a full meal and dessert on the table behind him. He'd taken advantage of the Pumpkin Patch's wing night while she'd been choking down reheated pasta. "It must have been very last minute. I never got a second call."

"I swear I left a message. Either way, you're here now. Let me by you some dessert."

"I'm with my friends."

"Well, introduce us, Evie-bear. The least I can do is apologize for interrupting your coffee klatch."

No, the least he could do was leave her in peace. "No, it's okay."

"Come on, introduce your dear, old dad," he wheedled. He smiled at her, the same goofy smile he'd give to her mom after they'd gone out for ice cream after school, and they'd come home with her too stuffed to eat dinner. Now she understood why her mother used to get so frustrated with them.

"We're in the middle of something. Why don't you call me later this week?" she asked, reluctant to compromise. She knew she was setting herself up for more disappointment.

Her dad patted her shoulder and stepped around her. "Hi, everyone. I'm Paul LeBlanc, father of the best tow truck driver in the province." His brown eyes, identical to her own, went to Gordon. "Are you my Evie's boyfriend?"

"Dad!" Eve turned on her heel and walked back to her seat, where she immediately stuffed a huge forkful of gingerbread cake into her mouth.

"No. I'm married," Gordon replied.

"Does your wife know you're out with a beautiful young woman?" her dad asked.

"Enough! Leave if you are going to insult my friends." Eve knew it was rude, but the acid churning in her stomach overruled her mother's voice in her head. He didn't get to walk in and take over her life like he'd been there all along. He definitely didn't get a say in her non-existent boyfriends.

"Evie, I'm just teasing. Is this a book club?"

Eve closed her eyes. She couldn't deal with him. Happily, she had friends with more tact than she did. "No, Mr. LeBlanc," Amanda said, "we're organizing a plan to find my daughter's dog, and we're tight on time. Do you mind?"

Her dad's smile faltered. "I heard about that at work. I'll let you get to it. My best to your daughter, and good luck on your search," he added before he walked out the door.

"I need more cake," Eve muttered. She hoped an obscene amount of cream cheese icing would drown out the memory of the last couple minutes.

"That was your father, right?" Amanda asked. She scratched her head under her toque. "The one who ditched you and your mom and your baby sister when you were young?"

Eve nodded and dipped her last piece of cake into the little ramekin of caramel sauce on the side of the plate.

"Weren't you supposed to have supper with him tonight?"

She was glad her friend was so smart. It was easier to answer questions than to speak the hurtful words. Eve nodded again.

"Last question. Did *you* cancel on *him*?"

A headshake this time.

Amanda scowled at his back, her white teeth bright against her dark skin. "Oh, that man!"

"Will you excuse me for a second?" Eve wasn't sure if she wanted to cry or scream, but she knew she didn't want to do either in front of her friends. She locked herself in the bathroom stall and took a deep breath. She shouldn't be upset. She wasn't the one who'd cancelled. She pulled out her phone. He hadn't called her a second time, and her incoming calls would prove it.

The message icon was engaged again. "Oh, no," she whispered. She gritted her teeth and pressed the button.

"Hi, Evie. My meeting was cancelled. Too many people called in sick. If it's not too late, can we still get together? I'll be at the Pumpkin Patch for dinner if you want to join me. I hope you get this. It's Dad, by the way."

So he hadn't lied. But she refused to let herself feel bad.

Jilly was waiting for her when she returned to the table. "Tow truck driver. You're a tow truck driver," the executive assistant said to her.

"You knew that," Eve said.

Jilly grinned. Her spiky, light brown hair gave her a pixie-like appearance. "Are you the driver that picked up my boss on the side of the road this afternoon? He texted me, and I arranged a tow, but they didn't tell me who they were going to send."

Eve nodded. "That was me. He's your boss?"

"You picked up Hot Nick?" Amanda asked excitedly.

"His name was Nick." The guy had been good look-ing, from what little she'd seen of him that wasn't buried under winter gear. She'd noticed how startling his blue eyes were against his blond hair, and how his toque had brought out the colour even more. "I don't know about hot. He had a cool truck," Eve admitted.

"Oh, please. Tim's pointed him out at work functions. He's hot," Amanda insisted. "I'm happily married, and I'm still saying that. Did he ask you out?"

"No! I just towed his truck."

"That boy is my protégé," George said, "therefore I won't comment on his hotness, but Nick needs to get out of the office. If he didn't ask you out, you should ask him on a date."

Eve pointed at George. "Don't you pile on, too. We're supposed to be looking for Bucky, not dates for me." She didn't say both scenarios had roughly the same chance of success. "Besides," she continued, "it's not like we're ever going to run into each other again." Not if he got his truck properly fixed, and from their short time together, Eve got the impression that Nick took his vehicle seriously.

"If he did ask you out, what would you say?" Amanda asked.

"Oh, for heaven's sake, it's never going to happen. Let's get back to Bucky sightings." Because the dog search was starting to have a better shot at a happy ending than she did.

Eve watched George and Jilly share a look, and it gave her a bad feeling. It grew when she caught Jilly flashing Amanda a "call me" sign behind her back.

She didn't trust any of them to let this go. Friends worried about each other, but true friends took action whether it was wanted or not. Eve felt the walls closing in on her. It was time to make a pre-emptive strike. She lied as hard as she could. "Seriously, he wasn't that cute."

She needed more cake.

3. NICK

THE WINTER EXTRAVAGANZA wasn't only a Santa Claus parade down December's Main Street on the first Saturday morning of its namesake's month. It was more than a combination craft show and bake sale. It was beyond a simple house decorating contest. It was the day that Christmas came to the town that was home to North Pole Unlimited, and he was honoured to be a part of it.

Nick's family had chosen December to establish their business a century earlier, when the town was a mere grain elevator stop at the end of a small railway line. Just south of the main hub to western Canada and the northern territories, it was ideally located for distribution. The fact it was less than an hour away from the American border was a bonus for the international arm his great-great-grandparents had envisioned for the future.

From the very beginning, North Pole Unlimited had concentrated on getting their goods where they needed to go. What started as a mail-order company had grown into a world-wide online store that provided the very best selections of gifts, decorations, and services for all occasions. They had catalogues for all the main holidays, of course, and birthday ideas for every age and hobby, but by far, they were best known for their Christmas offerings. Business doubled every week from the first of November to New Year's Eve.

This being the first week of December meant they were heading into the busiest month of the year with all its accompanying extra seasonal workers, who fell under Nick's Human Resources sphere.

But all that was incidental next to the Winter Extravaganza. Nick knew where his priorities lay.

He'd grown up in December. As a kid, today was one of his top ten days of the year, Christmas and his birthday topping the list. It rated just under Canada Day—fireworks, barbecues, and games along the beach of the Red River—and above St. Valentine's Day, because he'd been without a date more years than not. Nick smiled when he considered how many of his childhood extravaganza traditions he'd brought forward into adulthood, no matter how busy he'd gotten at work. He still took the time to spread holiday decorations around his house and hang twinkling lights in his window that could be seen from the street. He didn't make snowmen for the yard competition anymore, but he always ensured the neighbourhood kids had a box of snow sculpture accessories to work with.

He also attended the craft show and bake sale every year. That was more business than pleasure. North Pole Unlimited was the event's major sponsor, and as one of the company's vice-presidents, he had to make an appearance. This year, he was escorting his grandmother through the various stalls.

It was Adelaide Klassen's first time at the extravaganza as a civilian after her retirement the year before, and from the grin on her face, she was thoroughly enjoying herself. The steely-haired lady patted him on his arm. "I'm going to visit with Jilly and the girls for a bit. Why don't you hit the bake sale and come back for me?" she asked.

When his assistant Jilly pulled a folding chair out of thin air and set it out so the women could have a good chat, he gave up. "I'll make the rounds and come back later," Nick said as they shooed him away from the Southern Manitoba Fibre Association table.

To be honest, he would have hit the bake sale in the smaller hall without her encouragement, but now he had an excuse. There was no way he was passing up plates of pre-made Christmas dainties. He told the bakers he bought from that he wanted to have desserts on hand for entertaining; they didn't need to know he purposely "forgot" to invite people over and ate them all himself at a party for one.

He couldn't be the only person who did that. Not everyone appreciated a good confetti square, and he couldn't in good conscience let them go to waste.

Half an hour and five trays later, Nick was grateful for the natural freezer as he locked his purchases in the cab of his truck. He returned to the community centre and made his way to the stage at the front of the auditorium where Mayor Rychuk waited for him.

"Good afternoon, Nick. Ready for the awards ceremony?" December's new mayor was two years into his first term, so events like the extravaganza were still new to him. His enthusiasm was refreshing.

"Hi, Leo. You've picked all the winners?" North Pole Unlimited offered first place and runner-up prizes for the best decorated yards and best under-eighteen designed costumes that had been in the parade the night before.

The mayor handed him the list. Nick scanned the entries. "Wow, four new winners this year," he noted. The Scott family had dominated the house decorating contest for the last four years, but they hadn't placed this time.

"There was some serious competition. Shall we get started?"

"Please."

Leo flicked the switch on the microphone standing in the middle of the stage. After he made his introductory remarks, he handed the mic over to Nick.

The room stilled, with a few quiet conversations interrupting the attentive silence. "Hi, everyone, I'm Nick Klassen from North Pole Unlimited. I'm very pleased to be the one to announce the winners of this year's December Winter Extravaganza Decorating Contests." He quickly called the winners of the parade costume competition to the stage and handed out the appropriate gift baskets.

The runner-up for the house decorating part was not present, so he set the basket aside. "Now for the big one. This year's winners for the house decorating competition are...Emily LeBlanc and Helen Gauthier!" He remembered this display. The duo had turned their porch into a basket by weaving garland through the spindles and had "spilled" ornaments all across their front yard. Every bush, barrel, and a few wire-framed shapes were wrapped in ribbons and lights.

A "woo-hoo" echoed through the gymnasium, and a blonde teenager approached the stage, pulling an older woman behind her. They looked familiar, and it took

Nick a minute to recognize the name. LeBlanc. They resembled his tow truck saviour from earlier in the week.

He handed the prize to the teen. Her knees bounced as she took the full weight of the basket. It was loaded with products from North Pole Unlimited's massive Christmas catalogue: games, gourmet snacks, winter wear, and a handful of things that could be stuffed in any stocking. He laughed when she awkwardly tried to shake his hand, then stood between her and her mother for photographs. "That was some amazing light work," he said to them.

"Thank you," Helen said. "Emily came up with the design last Christmas. We've been working on it for a year."

"It's a magnificent display," Mayor Rychuk said. "Congratulations."

After the photos, Nick wormed his way through the crowded aisle of the craft show to find Adelaide ready to go. In addition to Jilly and a couple others he recognized, his grandmother was standing with a woman. "Nick, dear, I'd like you to meet Laurel Murphy. She's the operations manager at Pearson's Dairy Farm by Brunkild."

Nick gave the new woman another look. Early thirties, pretty brown eyes, no rings. Yes, it was another set-up. "Nice to meet you," he said politely, because it wasn't Laurel's fault.

Adelaide handed him a cellophane covered tray. "Here. Laurel made chocolate covered peanut butter balls for the bake sale. I bought the last ones before they all disappeared." She turned to her innocent mark. "My grandson loves peanut butter," she continued.

"Thanks, Gran. I'm sure they're delicious." He

needed to get out of here before he found himself hog-tied and headed for the altar. "We have to get going."

Laurel walked with them to the parking lot. They saw her to her car and continued down the row to his truck. He and Adelaide shivered on the bench seat as he fought to turn the engine over. This time, unlike his problems on the highway, he wasn't even getting a signal from the battery. "Unbelievable," he muttered. He'd just been given the all-clear from Webster's Garage.

He twisted the key in the starter a fourth time and whacked the steering wheel in frustration. Then he spied a wreath-decorated solution on the other side of the lot. He pulled out his phone and hoped salvation was still in the building. *"Please say you're working today. We're in the parking lot,"* he texted to Eve.

She responded immediately. *"Be right there."*

He looked up from the screen at a sudden knock at his window. Laurel stood right outside his door. "Need a hand?"

"Perhaps Laurel can help us out," Adelaide suggested.

And leave him trapped with his grandmother and her match-making choice? No thanks. He opened his car door. "One second, please," he said to Laurel. "Eve!" he shouted, as he saw her exit the community center.

Her head turned, and she headed their way. "Hello, again, Nick. Please tell me you were joking about breaking down again," she called.

He raised his hands helplessly.

Laurel generously stepped up to the plate. "I can drive you home if you're stranded," she offered.

He made his choice. "Thank you, but I need to stay with my truck. It would be great, though, if you could drop off my grandmother. She lives a few kilometres out of town, but it's in your general direction."

Laurel looked from Eve to him. She nodded once. "No problem. I can take Adelaide home. She's a hoot. Are you sure you don't want a ride?" She paused to admire his truck. "You could repay me with a ride in yours once it's up and running."

"Thanks for taking her. I—we—really appreciate it."

His grandmother grumbled as she climbed out of the cab. He caught "ungrateful" and "never get grandkids" but the rest was too muffled in her scarf to hear. What was perfectly audible? "Eve, how did we get lucky enough to have you on hand?"

"Didn't you see me inside? I had a suspicion that Emily would win with what she did to the house. Plus, I bought all my Christmas presents. Spoiler—everyone is getting hand-knit slippers this year," Eve said with a laugh. "Are you sure you don't want to wait a minute? I doubt this will take long."

His crafty grandmother shook her head. "No, dear. I'm fine. Laurel is going to drive me home. You stay with Nick. He needs all the help he can get." Laurel took her arm and led them to her own vehicle. The last thing Nick heard was, "Would it be an imposition to make a stop? My other grandson lives in town..."

He laughed. He wasn't even going to text Noel to warn him.

Eve slapped her hands together, her large, black leather mitts sounding like a mini-thunder clap. "Do you want to pop the hood and we'll see what's wrong with your baby this time?"

"Her name is Clementine."

4. EVE

CLEMENTINE. It suited the old-timey truck. Eve wondered if Nick's grandfather had been the one to name it or if he had. The grandfather, she thought. The name wouldn't have occurred to Nick, who was a few years older than her own twenty-five.

The hood weighed a ton. When she finally got it braced open, it took her half a second to spot the problem. "Your battery cables are disconnected."

"Excuse me?"

"Cables. Battery. Disconnected." She pointed to the heavy clips laying uselessly to the side of the battery prongs. While she was there, she checked the dipstick. Gordon must have changed the oil after she'd dropped Clementine off, because the viscous liquid was clear and high on the stick.

Eve pulled off her mittens and quickly reconnected the clips to the battery. She didn't need to take off the thin gloves she wore inside her mitts. The thin acrylic knit kept her skin off the freezing metal but left her fingers nimble enough to manipulate the finicky handles. The gloves didn't do anything for the cold, but she was quick enough that her mittens were still warm inside when she pulled them back on. "Want to try it again?"

Nick slid behind the wheel, and the engine turned over on his first try. He closed the door to let it run. "I don't suppose they normally pop off?"

"No." Wiggle off and end up on top of the battery? Highly unlikely. Disconnect and set itself neatly to the side? No chance.

"Gran," he growled.

"What?"

"I think..." He shook his head. "Never mind. Let's just say I owe you a huge favour."

She saw a familiar figure stop beside her mother and sister, who were coming out the community centre's main doors. "If you can teleport, I'll take you up on that favour right now."

"Is that your dad?" At her surprised look, Nick continued. "Once my grandmother mentioned his name, I remembered him talking about you in the lunch room. Not always by name, but he talks about you a lot."

It was too bad her father didn't seem to want to talk *to* her. She glanced over her shoulder again. He'd spotted her and was headed their way. "If you want to make your escape, now is the time." Heaven knew she did. "Shoot, too late."

"Hi, Paul." Nick was polite, but not welcoming. He stood next to her without touching her. Almost like he was silently offering backup if she wanted it.

"Hello, Nick. Hi, Evie."

"Hi, Dad."

Her father looked at the two of them and Clementine's exposed engine. "Need a hand?"

"It's okay. I took care of it." To Eve's surprise, he didn't try to slide by her to look for himself. She unhooked the hood and let it shut with a *clang*.

"I told you she's the best," Paul bragged.

"You did. That's twice she's helped me out," Nick agreed.

"Evie, I thought you said you weren't working this weekend."

She turned away to drop the hood back in place. "I'm not."

"I saw her in the parking lot and begged for help when my truck wouldn't start. My grandmother was with me. I didn't want to leave her stranded." Nick moved a little closer but still didn't touch her.

Eve smiled behind her scarf. Nick seemed to understand that she didn't want to have this conversation. She'd call it more than even if he helped her get out of it.

"If she helped you on her day off, the least you could do is buy her a coffee," Paul said.

Was it reasonable to hope the ground would swallow her whole if it was under six inches of packed snow?

"You're absolutely right, Paul. What do you say we get out of here, Eve?" Nick asked. His blue eyes were trying to tell her something, but she didn't understand.

What she did know was that he was offering her a way out. "Sounds great, Nick."

"Hop in. I'll bring you back to your truck afterward."

She lifted her chin, then gave her father a jaunty wave. "Bye, Dad."

Eve waited until they were out of the parking lot and down Burlington Road before she spoke. "Thanks for getting me out of there. If you want to loop around, you can drop me back off. He's probably gone now."

"Absolutely not." Nick's vehement refusal shocked her. "There is no way that is not getting back to my gran. She has spies everywhere. If I said I was taking you out for coffee and I don't have witnesses to prove I did it, I'm a dead man. Dead with a capital D. Please save me from grandmotherly disapproval."

She laughed. "It looks like we're both stuck. Okay, you can buy me a coffee. Do you want to hit the Pumpkin Patch or Norma's?" she asked.

"The Pumpkin Patch," he said, much to her delight. Their dessert case was always full, and their espresso machine was never down. He looked like all that and had good taste, too.

"Since I'm saving you from Adelaide, you can buy the coffee. Since you saved me from my dad, I'll buy the treats."

"Deal."

Eve spent the rest of the short drive admiring the interior of his truck. The way the steering wheel sat atop a long pipe bracketed to the dashboard spoke of the simple engineering of the age. The extra-long gearshift stretched to the floor. The lack of all things digital shocked her every time she looked at the dashboard. "How many times has that odometer rolled over?" she asked.

"At least three. Possibly four."

It was in the ninety-thousands again. The Klassen men had taken very good care of their baby. "Clementine is a real beauty."

Nick patted the steering wheel. "She really is. I started begging my grandfather for permission to drive her the second I got my learner's license. He and my grandmother gifted me the truck on my first day with

North Pole Unlimited so I could drive myself to work. I've taken care of her ever since.

The Pumpkin Patch had two full tables, not unusual for this time of day. Eve wrapped her hands around her mug as soon as it arrived, trying to bank the heat for the next time she was out in the cold. "Why are you afraid of your grandmother?" she asked.

Nick cringed at her question. "I'm not afraid of her. I'm just a little tired of her constant matchmaking. She says I spend too much time at the office, which is hilarious, considering she was worse than I was until she retired last year. She wants me to find a 'balance' in life." He made the air quotes for emphasis, and his frustration continued to tumble out of his mouth. "Gran thinks that means me having a girlfriend, and 'since I'm not doing the job myself'"—there went the air quotes again— "she's taken it upon herself. You got a quick taste of it when you drove me to her place. She introduced Laurel to me five minutes before you met her in the parking lot. She probably has one waiting upstairs at her house for the next time I show up."

Eve got it. Parental, or grandparental, interference was no fun at all. "I know the feeling. At least you know what you're getting with your grandma. I have no idea what my dad is capable of."

"What's the deal with him? Does he think you're working too hard, too? Because you must be hopping at this time of year between dead batteries and people sliding into ditches," Nick said. He tugged a paper napkin from the dispenser on the table and brushed the crumbs from his cookie back onto the plate.

"I have no idea. We haven't been close for years. For

some reason, he's decided now is the time to change that."
She poked at her butter tart.

Nick frowned. "Ouch."

"He doesn't mean any harm, but he seems to think
I'm still his nine-year-old Evie-bear. I haven't been her in
fifteen years." Eve sighed. She shouldn't be dumping this
on a guy she'd just met. "Sorry, you don't need to hear
this."

"Don't apologize. I'm happy to listen in return for
grabbing onto you like a life preserver when my grandmother tried to invite me and Laurel to her place for tea."
He pushed himself away from the table. "Excuse me for
one minute."

He didn't go to the bathroom, as she expected.
Instead, he strode over to the dessert counter. He chatted
with the waitress for a moment, pointed at something she
couldn't see, and raised two fingers before he returned.
"Want to avoid familial disappointment for a while
longer?"

The waitress scurried over with two fresh-from-the-
oven cookies, including an oatmeal chocolate chip one
with caramel drizzle on top.

"Sure. Tell me all about Clementine. Because I think
I want to buy her twin sister." Eve already knew she had
to add a 1940 Ford pickup to her wish list to Santa.

Nick smiled, and it warmed her as much as her coffee.
"The first repair I paid for was for a new clutch because I
burned out the old one learning how to shift gears. I was
fifteen and a half with a learner's permit," he said as he
settled into his seat for what sounded like a great story.

Eve leaned closer in anticipation.

5. NICK

"I HEAR you had a date this weekend," Jilly said as soon as Nick entered his office the following Monday morning. She brushed her brown bangs out of her eyes. "Want to share any PG details?"

Now he knew what his gran had been doing at the craft show; she'd been recruiting volunteers. "Please, Jilly, don't start. I had fourteen emails waiting for me when I got up this morning. For the love of Christmas bonuses, please tell me there is coffee in the staff lounge. My office pot is broken."

The benefit of having a VP's office was supposed to be the perks contained within it. In addition to the broken coffeemaker, Nick had a treadmill in the corner, which he'd bought, a sixty-inch television with a full cable package, which he'd had installed, and a singing, stuffed bass on a plaque his predecessor had left on the wall as a practical joke before he left. Nick hadn't disposed of it yet. It was growing on him.

"I'm not asking for gossip. Personal gossip is for small-minded individuals. Your dating life affects your happiness and Adelaide's happiness, both of which, in turn, affect my happiness, so this is, in fact, a business matter. Who is she? Is it serious? What's her name?"

"Jilly," he growled in warning.

"Spill."

Jilly Lewis was an executive assistant without equal. Nick had inherited her with the position of VP of Human Resources as she'd worked for his predecessor for close to a decade. Nick wouldn't have appeared half as competent as he had in his first year without her. On the flip side, the same experience that made him look good in front of his staff also meant Jilly knew everybody and provided background on them to give him an edge. Nick dreamed of having a network that delivered information like hers. Except when it was information about him.

He stifled a yawn. "Okay. Yes. I am in a new relationship. We spent all of Sunday morning in bed together. Her name is Pillow. We decided we're going to be exclusive. Did you bring me any coffee?" he asked hopefully.

"You're hopeless. There's fresh coffee in the break room."

He never made it that far. December in December was always nonstop work, but the morning had been nonstop emergencies. A brutal Alberta Clipper had stranded all of North Pole Unlimited's deliveries in the west. The tremendous winds were blowing a previous storm's grainy snow around on the ground, resulting in closed sections of the TransCanada Highway from the Alberta-Saskatchewan border east to Winnipeg.

If NPU trucks couldn't move, their goods couldn't be delivered. No deliveries meant panicked calls from the company's warehouse operators. If Nick wasn't reassuring them, he was dealing with stranded truckers who were looking for advice on hotels nearby where they could wait out the storms.

He couldn't control the weather, so he tried to predict it. With the Weather Channel playing in the background, he crossed his fingers and declared to one and all that the storm would pass by the end of that afternoon and deliveries would only be a day behind.

Thankfully, Jilly took mercy on him and kept his coffee mug full as she continued to forward calls to him.

It was well past noon before he got a moment to breathe.

Jilly popped into his office and dropped a brown paper bag on his desk. "This is insane!"

"You're not kidding." But the insanity didn't explain the bag. "What's this?" he asked.

"I ordered you lunch. You have fifteen minutes before the staff meeting, and Kristin warned me it's going to run long."

Nick double-checked the clock on the wall. His ever-efficient assistant was right; he'd never have time to go out and return with lunch. He wouldn't even have time to make it to the cafeteria. "Thanks, Jilly."

His phone pinged with an incoming text. "*Any more trouble with Clementine?*" He smiled; he hadn't expected to hear from Eve again.

"Good news?" Jilly asked.

"Unexpected hello from a friend."

She peeked over his shoulder and grinned when she saw the name. "You should text your secret girlfriend," she said before she left again.

"I take back my thank you!" he yelled at her disappearing form.

The sandwich took the edge off his hunger, but Nick stopped dead when he saw the paper taped under the Logistics Department sign. He pushed open the door and strode to the unit's shared administrative assistant. "Do you have any chocolate left?"

Kristin Gillam, often Jilly's partner-in-crime on the gossip circuit, nodded. "That fundraising poster is working wonders for my daughter's band trip." She pointed to a box on the corner of her desk.

"Nick, come on, we're going to be late," Decker Harkness yelled from the hallway.

Nick grabbed a box of chocolate-covered peanuts and a caramel bar before he dropped a ten-dollar bill on Kristin's desk and raced away.

The meeting kept to the agenda. All the other department heads were as busy as he was, and nobody had a second to waste. He returned to all the work he'd neglected that morning, and the calls which had piled up during his meeting.

Jilly bustled in with another stack of papers. "It's not stopping today."

Seconds later, she was back. "Sorry, Nick, I can't stay. I have to pick up Dan from a volleyball tournament."

Nick blinked. It was a normal statement in the fall semester; Jilly's son was an ace player and travelled to tournaments all over the province. But she usually didn't leave until four o'clock to collect him. He looked at the clock and it was ten after. "It's fine. Drive safely. I hope Dan did well."

"He always does," the proud mother said.

When Nick looked up again, it was pushing seven o'clock. The highways had all re-opened, and things were finally moving again. He still had a full inbox, but he decided to call it quits for the day. A new message arrived before he could turn off his monitor. From Jilly.

"You don't have to go home but you can't stay here. Good night."

Not a minute later, his desk phone rang. His hand hovered over the receiver; he recognized the number. "I'm going out tonight," he said aloud. There, now he had plans if she asked.

He picked up. "Hi, Gran."

"Nick, you're still at work." She had a movie playing in the background, likely one of her hundred holiday DVDs.

"I was on my way out the door and had to come back and answer the phone," he joked.

"What are you doing tonight? Why don't you come over for a late supper?" she offered. "That nice Laurel from Saturday is coming over to collect some craft supplies. You two could have a chance to get to know each other."

He knew it! "I already have plans for tonight, Gran, but thank you."

"With a girl?"

She never quit. While an admirable trait for a CEO, it wasn't the same in the personal arena. "Possibly," he fibbed.

"What are you doing?" she asked.

"Going to the pub," Nick decided on the spot. He was dead tired and had no desire to go home and cook himself a meal.

"I supposed that's almost as good as spending the evening with a gorgeous, fascinating young woman at my place. At least you won't be in the office all night," she conceded.

"I was truly on my way out the door."

His stomach rumbled so loudly his grandmother heard it over the phone. "Oh, my goodness. Get out of there and get something to eat. I love you, Nick."

"Love you, too, Gran."

He didn't move after he hung up. She was right. He needed a life outside of work. His best friend Hollis found a balance on a mountaintop where he met his current girlfriend. NPU's new security chief was another example of newfound domestic bliss; no matter how busy Decker got, the man always had time for his fiancée. On days like this, Nick saw the appeal in putting in the effort to find that special somebody and make it happen.

But not tonight.

Nick began a slow scroll through his contacts list. Tim Hill was probably home enjoying time with his family, relaxing now that his daughter was in remission.

Decker Harkness had a standing Monday date night with Joy.

Dave Block. Nick paused at that name. Dave was still single, as far as he knew. The IT manager was also a rabid hockey fan, and there was a Jets game on television that night. He quickly sent a text asking if Dave wanted to meet at the bar to watch the game.

"Sorry, Nick, out with my girlfriend tonight."

Dave had been single as long as Nick knew him. *"Girlfriend? Who?"*

"Tasha. Jilly introduced us."

"Next time," Nick texted back. He stared at the email

from Jilly and wondered if she knew what he'd do. She was so good at her job he wouldn't put it past her.

Too bad. He still wasn't cooking. He could go to Garland's Pub by himself. At least he'd be sure to enjoy the company.

6. EVE

EVE DIDN'T RECOGNIZE the car parked in front of her mother's house when she pulled into the driveway for their supper and show night. They ate and caught up on the previous week. Afterwards, they moved to the living room to watch the latest episode of whichever baking competition show was running. Currently, it was the Cross-Canada Christmas Kitchen Contest.

Her mom or sister usually made a Crock-Pot meal; Eve supplied the desserts, because hard experience had taught them the folly of watching a baking show without having goodies in the house. Today, Eve had cheated and brought a tray from the previous weekend's bake sale instead of making her own. She'd never make homemade brownies anyway.

It was a good thing she'd planned ahead, because she hadn't had time to breathe, let alone spend time baking. She'd had an everything-goes-wrong day.

First, she'd lost ninety minutes on a wild dog chase. Gordon had received a call that there'd been a retriever sighting at the campground by the river. "It makes sense," he'd said. "There are lots of places Bucky could take shelter. Plus, the dog knows the area. The Hills have camped there for years. Can you check it out?" he'd requested.

It was easier said than done. The entrance to Two Pines Beach Campground was off the plowed highway, but the lane itself hadn't been cleared. Eve made it about half a kilometer before she'd decided to go the rest of the way on foot. Some of the road was blown clear; other parts had thigh-high drifts she struggled through.

When she'd finally made it to the campground itself, she saw a glimpse of gold peeking out from behind the office cabin. She tromped through more snow to get there, only to catch another glimpse behind the bathrooms. She finally located it behind one of the permanent trailers.

There was no dog; it was a gold hoodie being blown around in the wind. The letdown was devastating. Eve had quickly called Gordon back. "You didn't let Amanda or Madison know about this tip, did you?" she'd demanded.

"No. No dog?"

"Not even close. I'm not seeing any animal tracks at all."

The garage owner sighed. "Sorry to send you all the way out there for nothing, Eve."

She'd pulled her damp pant leg away from her leg. "Not your fault, Gordon. We had to check." But what a waste of time and energy and hope it had been.

Eve had been halfway through changing her pants in a gas station bathroom when she'd gotten another assignment. This time, when she'd arrived to pull a car out of the ditch, she'd discovered the driver had melted enough snow to form a puddle exactly where she needed to kneel down to hook the chain. There went her back-up set of jeans. When the vehicle was finally back on the road, the panicked teen had begged Eve to let her drive home despite the facts both headlights were broken and it was missing the front bumper.

Now all Eve wanted was an evening full of warm chili and mindless television.

The second she walked through the front door she knew she wasn't going to get either. "Did you get my message that there would be four of us tonight?" her mother called from the kitchen.

"I did, Mom, and I brought enough dessert." What Eve hadn't known was the fourth setting at the table would be for her father. Her mother's very ex-husband.

Her sister Emily sat across from their dad. "We saved you your seat," she said.

Emily's eyes said more than that. Eve was aware Emily had been in contact with her dad for the last four years: emails and video-chats while he was working out of the province, and lunches since he'd returned to December.

Eve didn't begrudge her sister's newfound closeness with Paul. She did resent being blindsided by his presence at an event that should have been safe for her. Her mom knew how she felt about her father.

The stilted, four-way conversation was excruciating, but for her mother and her sister, she gave it her best shot. "I had a call out today on Operation Retriever, but it was another dead end. We promised Madison we'd keep looking till the new year, but even she is getting discouraged," Eve reported.

Emily's blonde head bobbed. Her sister had decided to go with coloured tips for her last year of high school. She started with blue. Now they were fuchsia. "Sightings on the Facebook page are dying off, too. It's too bad. Do you think Santa will bring her a new puppy for Christmas? I've been doing some research and I found a breeder to recommend to Amanda."

"That's sweet of you," her dad said.

"It is," her mom agreed. "I don't know if Madison would be open to the idea of a new pet. She might need more time. Keep that name in your back pocket, though. They might want it in the spring."

"Okay," Emily agreed.

Her sister was a great kid. Eve was always proud of her, but that pride doubled when Emily did something like this. It wasn't enough for Emily that she was an excellent student who already had conditional acceptance letters to three different universities and was on the school's track and field team. She also did enough community service to have an entire page of character references; Amanda Hill was one of many. Her sister was going places, and she deserved it.

"How was school today?" Paul asked.

Emily stuck out her tongue. "We had a biology test. Fifteen percent of our final. I studied like crazy, but I think I did okay. Hopefully, I can make up some marks since labs are worth ten percent. Our final exam is in a month." She crossed her eyes and laughed. "I'm trading bio tutoring with Dan for history."

"He has time to give tutoring? With his schedule?" her mom asked.

"He has to make time. He's desperate to get into the U of T political science program, and he needs help with history. Our schedules are lighter next semester, thank goodness."

Her father looked at her mom. "Dan?"

Eve saw steam. Was he really questioning her judgment right in front of her? "Dan Lewis," Eve said before her mom could. "You probably know his mom, Jilly. She's Nick's executive assistant. Dan's a great friend." Friend, but not boyfriend. He was the president of the high school's GSA, so everyone at the table except her father knew digging for romantic intentions was a waste of time. Dan was vice-president to Emily's president of the local Loki fan club.

"Eve." Her mother said her name as a sigh.

"Yes, mom?" She kept her smile plastered on her face.

When a phone beeped, all three women looked at the coffee table in the living room. They had a no-phones-at-the-kitchen-table rule to avoid interruptions to their meals.

Emily made it to the living room first. "Eve, it's yours."

It didn't take long for her to reply. "Work. I've got to go," she offered in explanation. She'd known interrupted meals were a hazard of the job, but sometimes they were more convenient than others. "Record the show for me, would you, Em? I'll come over and watch it later this week, so no spoilers."

Eve didn't want to leave with her mother annoyed at her, even though the annoyance was mutual, so she capitulated a bit on her way out the door. "Great stew, Mom. Thanks for talking me up at work, Dad. Nick said you were complimentary." There. That was pleasant and, as a bonus, true. She still would have been sent out as the closest on-call emergency tow no matter what, but people hearing her name could lead to other business.

"I want to support you. Having your own business is challenging."

"I appreciate the word of mouth. Enjoy the brownies!" she said on the way out the door.

The temperature had dropped as soon as the sun set, and the mercury continued to fall. She quickly jumped the car in the elementary school's parking lot, then cautioned the driver to cruise around for at least fifteen minutes before turning the engine off in order to give the battery a chance to recharge. Eve checked her watch. She could be back at her mom's and jump into the show by the first commercial break.

But she didn't want to deal with Paul again.

She tried to remember the last time she'd had an evening to herself with no plans. Her laundry was done, her fridge was full, and her apartment was clean. There was no reason to go home. So she didn't. Eve slowly chugged through December, enjoying the lights, and made her way to Garland's Pub.

The pub was attached to the hotel but not part of it. There was a jukebox in the corner, which Eve hadn't heard in years. A dozen TV screens lined the walls and played hockey, baseball, and football according to the season. Since it also hosted bachelor and bachelorette parties, they painted the interior annually. The carpet was replaced every four or five years, the tables didn't wobble, and the chairs and stools were recovered on a regular basis to keep things fresh.

Since the Canadian football season was over, the place was rocking with rowdy hockey fans. This early in the season, playoff talk was still a possibility, so the local fantasy draft was out in earnest, filling four tables in the corner.

What looked like a birthday night out occupied another two. The rest but one were filled with groups of three and four; from the bits and pieces of conversations she overheard, they were waiting for trivia night to start.

Eve weaved her way through the crowd to the lone table with a single occupant and rested her hand on the back of an unoccupied chair.

7. NICK

"HEY, THERE, IS THIS SEAT TAKEN?"

Nick knew that voice. It had saved him twice in the last week. He turned away from the game playing on the TV screen in the corner and spotted Eve in red again. But not Santa red.

"Are you trying to cause a riot? Wearing that in here?" he asked. Because the woman in front of him was in a Montreal Canadiens sweatshirt in the middle of a bar full of Winnipeg Jets fans in blue. Talk about waving a red flag in a room full of bull-headed fans.

Eve looked down at her chest. "Hello? Daughter of a LeBlanc and a Gauthier. Did you think there was a chance I wouldn't have been raised a Habs fan?" She patted the back of the chair again, and he nodded. He hadn't seen any friends he could join, so he'd found a table and indulged in a spectacular shepherd's pie from the pub's kitchen.

Mikki, the waitress for their half of the pub, pointed at her. "What do you want, traitor?" Mikki said it with a smile, and Eve laughed in return.

"My usual, and a bag of barbecue chips."

Nick took a second look at her while she ordered. Eve's bright cheeks gave her away. Her drink order of straight ginger ale confirmed it. "Are you always working?" he asked.

"Honestly, some days it feels like it." She drained the glass and Mikki was right there with a refill. "But as of six tomorrow morning, I'm not on call for the next three days. In a row," she added in mock excitement. "I may not move from my sofa."

"I'm jealous."

"If you want to play hooky, I'm binge-watching three different versions of Pride and Prejudice," Eve told him.

"Pride and Prejudice and Zombies?" he asked. Not that he had watched that version, either. A day full of historical dramas sounded like his own personal hell, even if there were zombies roaming the English countryside.

"Four," she amended. "I need to turn off my brain."

Mikki reappeared beside them with a fresh drink for him. "You picked the wrong night for that. It's trivia night. We're starting"—she checked the clock on the wall behind the bar—"in seven minutes."

"I've never done a trivia night," Nick said. He'd seen them, watched the questions flash on the television screens, and muttered answers under his breath if he knew them, but he'd never officially played.

"They're a hoot!" Eve cocked her head and gave him a look. "Want to play? We have time to join. Unless you have to go?"

He should leave. He could use an early night for a change. Work wasn't going to get less crazy, but he'd had a hot supper and now was sitting with a woman who'd made him laugh more in two minutes than he had all day. "Sure."

They took Mikki up on her offer and she handed them an answer sheet. They agreed to the pub rules—no electronic devices, no calling a friend—and they were off and running.

Right into a brick wall. They were out of the plane without a parachute. Up the creek without a paddle.

Because despite all of Eve's excitement, she sucked at trivia.

He was worse.

"Lois and Clark!" He scrawled his answer on the sheet, fending off Eve's feeble attempts to snatch the pen from his hand.

"It. Is. Not. Lois and Clark. That's. Superman," she grunted as she went for the paper again.

"No. They were the mapmaking duo who mapped America."

The buzzer sounded. "The answer is Lewis and Clark."

He was close. "I don't suppose we get partial credit."

Eve laughed. "Why would they start now?"

They were getting trounced. Embarrassingly. Thoroughly. The second worst team was still beating them by a dozen points. If the questions weren't sports—particularly hockey—related for Nick, or cars for Eve, they didn't have a clue. His high school history and geography teachers would be so disappointed in him. At least Eve guessed correctly at some of the art and literature questions.

When her last guess got them their fifth point of the night, she leaned over and whispered in his ear. "I'll bet you're pretty impressed with me right now, aren't you?"

"Very."

"I watched the movie version."

"Of *Anna Karenina*? How bored were you?"

"The   only-other-thing-on-television-was-curling bored."

After the next question, he asked, "Were you bored enough to watch a documentary on scientists of the twentieth century?"

"There was one, but I watched curling instead."

Nick hadn't laughed so hard in ages. Two hours later, when the final scores were tallied, he and Eve had lost by an unprecedented fifty points. "You're right. This was fun."

He noticed a stain on the cuff of her sleeve when she reset her ponytail for the third time than night. She tended to run her fingers through her hair when she was stymied by a question. "It was. We should do it again sometime," she said.

"When all the other teams need to feel better about themselves?"

"We'll call it public service," she joked back.

He blamed the late hour and his busy day for not realizing what he'd said until the next morning. He'd made a date. With Eve. In public. It wasn't an official date, but it would be more than enough to set off the gossips.

He was right.

"I guess you won't be working late next Monday," Jilly said with a grin. "Aren't trivia nights fun?" She commented no further, but she left a cup of coffee on his desk.

As nutty as Monday was, the rest of the week got progressively worse. He came in for a few hours on Saturday but headed straight home early in the afternoon.

Christmas season or not, people still needed to sleep; that was all Nick did on Sunday.

It was enough, barely, to get him through Monday. When five o'clock rolled around, he could have gone home, had supper, and fallen right into bed.

But he preferred to lose at trivia. He hoped Eve had the same idea.

8. EVE

SHE HADN'T HAD an evening call-out for two nights in a row. Eve crossed her fingers to encourage her good fortune to last. She'd had time to get home, shower, and change before she headed to Garland's Pub for a...

Her brain stuttered. She was hoping to run into Nick for trivia night again. It wasn't a date, but going out with a friend was still an excuse to dress up a bit more than usual.

She held the adorable Christmas sweater Emily had given her last year in front of her and stared in the mirror. It was cream coloured, except for the dainty ring of green holly and red berries below the collar. It took her a second to decide to whip off her sweatshirt and replace it with the knit sweater. Her opportunities to wear her gift were limited, so she wasn't going to waste one. Eve added a cranberry leather belt, and green glass, teardrop earrings and headed out.

When she arrived, she discovered they were already on the team list. "Team Awesome Trucks?" she asked as she slipped onto the bar stool beside Nick's.

He looked good. Tired, but so did most of the others in the pub. Since they all worked at North Pole Unlimited, it made sense. Their busy season matched hers. He offered her a bright smile as he helped her take off her ski jacket. "Mikki needed a name. It was the first thing that came to mind."

"It's accurate," she agreed with a laugh.

This week, Amanda and Tim Hill sat at the table next to them, and the couple was quickly joined by Ginger Johansson and Clara Dempsey, two local business owners. "We heard what happened last week. We want to see if it was a fluke or if you two are really as awful as the stories say," Ginger said.

"We really are," Eve told her. "But we're going to double our score this week, right, Nick?"

"It won't be hard," Nick joked. He laid his hand on her arm to get her attention. "Are you on call tonight?"

She nodded. "It couldn't be helped."

"Hey, if anybody gets working a lot, it's me." He ordered two ginger ales from Mikki, and added a side order of French fries. When she nodded, he requested ketchup, as well. "I have a theory that we did poorly last week because we didn't have any brain food."

"I'll take any excuse I can get."

"Maybe you should order two," Tim suggested.

"Keep your eyes on your own sheet, Hill." Eve and Nick and the other teams didn't have time for any more banter when Mikki called the game to order.

Nick offered her a high five after their sixth correct answer of the night. "New high score!" he crowed.

Eve laughed and immediately regretted it. They'd laughed so hard and so often in the last hour, her ribs hurt. What made it even funnier is that they truly tried to come up with the correct responses, not simply blurt out the first things that came to mind. They couldn't seem to help themselves.

The iconic boat in a 1970s hit was the Orca, not the Minnow—*Jaws*, not *Gilligan's Island*. It was still a fish. How were they supposed to know a show that ended decades before they were born was made in the 60s and not the 70s?

Zeus's wife was Hera, not Juno. They'd confused the pantheons.

Eve still felt they deserved the point for claiming Mauna Kea was the highest mountain on the planet. The question didn't specify the whole mountain had to be above sea level. Tim Hill had given the same answer, so he was on her side for that appeal. They'd both lost, much to the amusement of the other teams.

Eve hadn't heard her phone buzz, but she checked for notifications anyway as they organized for the next round. She had a message waiting. "Shoot," she muttered under her breath. She didn't want to leave.

"Work?" There was no accusation in Nick's voice. Just curiosity.

Amanda and Tim were too deeply engrossed in their own conversation to overhear them. Eve leaned into Nick anyway. "No. Do you know about the Hills' missing dog?"

"Bucky? Yes, I've seen the notices around town."

She didn't want to do this. She was having a great time with Nick. "I'm on the search committee, and we have a sighting that needs to be checked out. Right now." She stared at the message again. Maybe she could ask Gordon to take this one. Or Joy. She could text Joy.

"Let's go." He pulled on his toque, the one that made his eyes look so blue.

"What?"

"We already beat our personal best. If we leave now, it'll still be low enough to beat next time." Nick lifted her jacket from the back of her stool. "I'm assuming you don't want Amanda and Tim to know where we're going?"

Eve slipped her arms into her sleeves. "Not until we have proof it's Bucky." Madison's parents had had enough ups and downs this past year to last a lifetime. Giving them what could be false hope was cruel. "You don't have to come. It's cold outside."

"I can't abandon my partner now. We're on a roll."

As they made their excuses for leaving the game early, Eve didn't receive any flak from the other players. They assumed she was on call for work, and nobody could begrudge a roadside rescue when it could be them next time.

The vents and rear window defroster quickly took care of the frost build-up on the wrecker's windows, and they drove into the dark winter night. "Hey, Emily, Nick and I are heading out to check on your tip," Eve said into the truck's speaker. They stopped at the turnoff to the kennel where Bucky was originally dropped off. "How certain are you?"

"Very," Emily said. "Penny saw him with her own eyes, but her kids are sick, so she couldn't go outside to chase after him. He's right there."

"Okay. Call Penny and tell her we're a few minutes away. If she has food or something that might help draw Bucky in, that would help. I'll call you when we're done." Eve's grin hurt her face. "This could be it!"

Nick covered her hand with his own and gave it a quick squeeze. "It would be a tremendous early

Christmas present. I don't think Madison would ask Santa for anything else."

The moonlight turned the snow-covered fields blue. There were sporadic lumps under the snow, bales of hay which were never picked up. They could provide some shelter for Bucky, but nothing that would help during the long cold snap they were experiencing. Lights shining through windows belied how empty the area looked. The buildings along this particular stretch of road outside of December provided plenty of places for a runaway canine to hide. Many of the garages, barns, and outbuildings were heated to various degrees. They'd all been searched, but if Bucky had returned to the scene of the crime, they might get lucky.

Penny George, the kennel owner, met them at the door with a pail of kibble in one hand and a runny-nosed toddler on her hip. "It was him. For certain. I saw Bucky on the far side of the outside exercise pens around back."

The sleepy fount of infection in her arms sneezed on her mother's throat. Penny closed her eyes. "Obviously, I couldn't go running after him. No matter how much I want to run far, far away right now." She pulled a hand-kerchief from her back pocket and dabbed at the side of her neck. "Good luck out there."

Eve and Nick circled the extension attached to Penny's triple garage, grateful that she kept the walkway clear. The snow inside the long, narrow run was well-trampled, but outside the chain link fence, Eve spotted a set of tracks. "Do those look golden retriever sized to you?"

"The only tracks I can identify are train," Nick said, his nose buried in his scarf. "They could be. Want to follow them?"

The trail led to a machine shop at the edge of the George property. A panel in the back lay half buried in the snow, leaving a small opening. Nick rattled the bucket. "Here, Bucky. Here, boy!"

Nothing. Eve's ears burned in the cold, but she didn't hear any movement in the dark. "Maybe he's sleeping someplace else."

The patch of trampled snow had a trail leading away from the house and shop, across a field of what would be wild grasses in the summer, and through a windbreak of poplar trees to the barn on the neighbouring property.

"Come here, Bucky. We have treats!" Eve drew out her plea in the singsong voice people used to call their pets.

Nick scoured the area with his flashlight. "In my oh-so-expert opinion, these tracks are fresh. I mean, they haven't been covered by new snow yet. They split toward the house and onto the next property. Who lives here?"

Eve spent every work day cruising the roads around December. If anyone knew, it would be her. She was the first to know about accidents, construction, and properties for sale. It was the last which was important tonight.

"This is the Shaw place. They use the buildings for storage, but nobody lives in the house anymore."

"That would explain why they didn't report Bucky hanging around." He slapped his hands against his thighs. "Bucky!"

There might have been a bark in the distance, or it could have been the creak of the trees bending in the wind, which was picking up by the minute. "I don't think we can do anything more tonight. At least now we know where to look," Eve said. She would have sounded more excited if she weren't freezing. "I'm tempted to dump a load of kibble here and at Penny's place, but I don't want to draw any critters." Inviting pests into someone's garage was nasty; raccoons, mice, and squirrels could all do massive amounts of damage over the winter.

"Let's find a couple sheltered places and leave it for him there. And then get inside. I hate to think a runaway dog is smarter than two creatures with opposable thumbs." Nick grabbed her hand and began pulling her back the way they'd come. Their boots squeaked in the snow as they double-timed it back to Penny's. They stopped to dump some kibble in the tree line.

Penny greeted them in a new shirt. "Well?"

"He's around. He's been staying next door by the looks of things. We'll be back to check it out in the daylight. If you want to put some food by the kennel fence, it might bring him back," Eve suggested.

"I'll do that. Are you going to call the Hills?"

Eve wanted to. Delivering good news would be the cherry on the sundae of a very good day. "First thing tomorrow. Let's let Madison have a full night's sleep. The poor kid will probably be bouncing off the walls after she hears." They'd be lucky if Madison didn't insist on coming out to the kennel and leading the search herself.

They drove back to town beaming. Eve pulled into Garland's Pub's parking lot. "That was way better than winning at trivia," she said.

"Not that we were winning, but I totally agree."

"Thanks for coming out with me."

Nick tugged down his scarf. "I wouldn't have missed it for the world. Are you going back tomorrow?"

"I'm not sure. The others will probably be out searching during the day," she said. Now that they knew where to concentrate their efforts, Operation Retriever would marshal all their forces.

"Same time next week?" he asked.

Eve nodded, not even stopping to think. "Sounds great."

9. NICK

IT TOOK him two days to realize he hadn't received a *"stop by and meet a lovely young woman who will be visiting at the same time"* call from his grandmother in the last week. They'd spoken on the phone, but Adelaide had restricted her comments to non-dating related topics.

Although, come to think of it, she had spent a lot of time asking about Clementine and her recent repairs. Which had led to him telling her about Eve reading Gordon the riot act about not hooking the battery cables back on properly.

Thinking of Eve, they hadn't confirmed their schedules to see if they were on for trivia the next week. He shot her a text and put the phone in his pocket, expecting a long wait time, especially if Eve was on the road.

Jilly scurried into the lunch room, still wearing her scarf. She set a paper bag on the table, opened it, and pulled out a cardboard bowl with a plastic lid, which she immediately pulled off and tossed in the sink. A cloud of steam erupted, bringing with it the savoury smells of homemade chicken soup.

"Where did you get that?" Nick asked.

"Norma's Buns. It's the special today. If you get the meal deal, they give you a drink and a free mini cinnamon bun for dessert, too." Jilly leveled a glare at him. "Don't even think of offering to buy it from me. It's mine."

His phone pinged with a response from Eve. *"Looking forward to it unless this cold kills me."* It was followed by an emoji blowing its nose. Nick hadn't known Eve long, but he'd never heard her complain. He had to assume she was hurting.

Jilly stared at him. "Why the frown?"

"Eve has a cold."

She nodded. "Ah, your secret girlfriend. How bad?"

"Pretty bad, I think."

Norma's chicken noodle soup was magic; the guys in the warehouse swore a bowl could cure a cold by the next morning. The clock on the wall said it was half past twelve. "I'm going to get some lunch. If I'm a little late, please compile the Q3 reports and I'll review them when I get back."

———

He hesitated, his finger hovering over the buzzer to Eve's apartment. He didn't even know if she liked soup. He took a breath and pressed the button.

Eve opened the door with a nose red enough to give Rudolph a run for his money. She was still in flannel pajamas—penguin-patterned ones, from what he could glean from the legs sticking out from under her thick bathrobe. "Please tell me your truck is okay," she rasped.

"Clementine is fine. You sounded like you could use

some TLC, though," he said. He held out the brown paper back. "Chicken noodle soup from Norma's."

"Yum. Thank you." She accepted the bag and waved him in. "You didn't have to."

"I need you well for our next trivia night. We need all the advantages we can get."

She laughed until it turned into a cough. "Ain't that the truth. Do you want some?"

"No thanks. It's for you." He looked around, soaking in the details of her apartment. Her walls were stuffed to the brim; paintings and prints of famous locations and buildings from all corners of the world filled every blank space. "Have you been to any of these places?" he asked.

"Not yet. How about you?"

"Some of them." A lot of them. His family believed in travelling whenever it was possible, and with the family business having connections around the globe, it had been easy enough to tag along on his parents' business trips when he was a kid. Now he was seeing them again on his own and realizing how little he'd appreciated the opportunities of his youth.

"Lucky." Eve sneezed three times in succession. "Sorry."

"When did you get the cold?"

"Tuesday. Probably from our wild-goose-slash-dog-chase the night before. I'm already over the worst of it. Thankfully, this seems to be a quickie. I need to go out for more tissues later, but I'll be back on my feet tomorrow. A couple more naps and I'll be good to go." She sneezed again. "The more I sneeze, the closer I am to the end. It's like my body is trying to shake the last of the cold, literally."

Nick didn't remove his hat or unzip his coat. "I won't keep you from your naps. I hope you feel better soon."

"Thanks," she said, "and thank you again for the soup."

He was back at work before Jilly had time to get bored with her stack of reports. He was pleased with himself. Eve seemed to truly appreciate the soup. He would have, too; he hated being sick. The miserable feeling of being stuck inside with barely enough energy for self-pity was never fun.

"Where's your soup?"

"I took it to Eve."

His assistant's grin almost split her face in two. "How is she?"

"Almost over her cold. I should stop by with tissues after work," he reported. "How are those reports coming?"

She lifted her head and pointed to his office. "The first batch is waiting for you."

Nick settled behind his desk. He lifted the receiver to ask Jilly a question without yelling through the closed door, but a glance at his phone indicated she was making a call. Stalling before he dug into the reports—he'd do anything to avoid the quarterly reports—he decided to check in with his grandmother and make sure she didn't need anything from town while she was still without her licence. When it went directly to voicemail, he hung up without leaving a message.

Then he heard Jilly's laugh through the door.

Jilly was reporting on his lunch stop at Eve's. To his grandmother. His assistant was the reason his gran's matchmaking attempts had petered off.

A small part of him resented the spying, but it was quickly overcome by an insane thought.

Totally bonkers. Completely unacceptable. And utterly brilliant.

He and Eve weren't dating. An unplanned trivia team-up and half of another game was not dating. Checking in on a friend was not a declaration of love. However, if the very appearance of it kept both his grandmother and Jilly at bay, he imagined what a couple well-placed hints could accomplish. Nothing definite, and absolutely nothing incriminating. He didn't have to lie. He just needed to offer a little misdirection to keep himself matchmaker-free till after the holidays.

It was the perfect plan.

10. EVE

NICK KLASSEN just jumped to her number one spot of favourite men on the planet. Not only had he saved her a trip to the grocery store, he had hand-delivered a care package of more soup, chewable vitamin C tablets, and tissues. Tissues *with lotion*. Her nose was in love with him.

When there was another knock half an hour later, she was at a loss as to who it could be. She'd already told her mother not to stop by; she had everything she could possibly need.

She absolutely did not expect her father to be at her door.

Eve had been fresh from the shower when Nick arrived. Now she had an afternoon's worth of sick sweat and rumpled hair. She didn't have the energy to worry about it.

"Hi, Dad."

"Hi, Evie. Can I come in?"

She stepped aside. She noticed how his head swiveled as he toed off his boots. He'd never been to her apartment before; he'd never asked if he could come over. The last time he'd seen where she lived, she had posters of well-scrubbed boy bands on her walls and stuffed animals on her bed. That wide-eyed little girl was long gone.

He perched on the edge of her sofa. The cushions were well-worn, but he wouldn't sink below the frame. "I didn't know you like to travel."

"I'm saving." Eve had seen most of southern Manitoba and a little of Saskatchewan and Northern Ontario, but that was it. She had plans, though, and a separate bank account that could take her to British Columbia in the summer for a weeklong vacation, or to Mexico the next winter if she kept on target.

"You didn't vacation with your mother and sister?"

"On what? All that child support you missed?"

Paul flinched. "It's too late to make a difference to you now, but I want you to know that I've made up those payments. At least Emily will have the opportunity." He sat straighter and took a deep breath. "I'm sorry I wasn't a good father."

Eve had no idea what to do with that. "Thanks?"

"I want you to know, when I left without a word when you were little, it had nothing to do with you. You were a great kid. Emily was a wonderful baby." He was still except for his hands. His fingers twisted over themselves like a ball of worms. "I was the problem. I was in a rush to have it all—the house, the family, the career—but I was too immature and stupid to realize I had to earn it."

She knew that. She hadn't understood it at the time, but when she looked back as an adult, the fights she'd overheard when she was in bed and her parents were in the kitchen had always been about her father's next great idea and her mother's insistence on stability. After he'd left, that had become her mother's primary focus. It was one of the reasons Eve was the way she was. "I don't ever remember you saying this before."

"Because I didn't. Back then, rather than step back and regroup when it got hard, I made excuses. When your mother argued with me and I couldn't deny her logic made sense, I threw a tantrum, whining she wasn't supportive enough. I wanted what I wanted when I wanted it and proclaimed to the world that if I couldn't have it all, I didn't want any of it. When the world didn't hand it over to me on demand, I left. Evie, I was the biggest fool on the planet."

She needed more tea to deal with this. "Why are you telling me now, Dad?"

"Because you are an adult and I owe you an apology."

"You owe Mom one first."

"I've been apologizing to her for years." He had a sheepish smile. Eve expected his voice to be bitter, but instead it held a little laughter. "She didn't tell you?"

"No." Eve wouldn't have listened to her anyway.

He nodded. "It took me a few years to grow up enough to realize what I'd done. What I'd thrown away. It took a couple more before I was in any position to try to make amends. Helen didn't trust me for a long time. She didn't want me in contact with you until she did. By the time she thought I was ready, you'd already moved out."

When he leaned forward, the light from the lamp caught every wrinkle on his face. Her dad was old. In all the photos she had of him, he was a young man, almost the same age she was now. He'd left fifteen years ago. That was a lifetime.

"I've been in contact with Emily for about four years. You didn't respond to my letters, and I wasn't going to push it when I lived a thousand miles away. But I'm here now to spend what time I can with you girls. Emily's going to university next year."

"What will you be doing?" With her younger sister gone, he wouldn't have much reason to stick around. He may have made peace with her mother, but Eve knew there was no going back in that relationship.

"I'm staying in December. I have a good job at NPU, and I'm mature enough to appreciate the stability I used to scorn. I'd like to spend this time getting to know you. Can we try to have dinner again, just the two of us?"

She didn't want to have to admit the truth. "I missed your message about meeting me at the restaurant after we ran into each other. I listened to it after you'd left the restaurant."

"I wondered about that. Thanks for telling me. I'm not going to stand you up again, Evie. I'll do whatever it takes to prove it to my little girl."

He was saying everything she wanted to hear. Everything she'd dreamed about since ten-year-old Eve understood that her daddy wasn't coming back. She knew that he'd been trying with Emily and doing a good job with her by all accounts. On the other hand, he was also the one who had broken Eve's heart in the first place. It wasn't as if she owed him anything. "I'm not that girl anymore, Dad. I'm an adult now. It's great that you're trying to be a dad to Emily, but I don't need one."

He nodded again, but the shadows highlighted his small frown. "How about a friend? Everybody needs friends."

People should be able to count on their friends. "Friends are a lot of work. Are you up for that?" She could do the work, for her sister, for her mother. Eve knew that if she had any kind of relationship with her father, Emily would appreciate it. Her little sister didn't need to feel guilty because she wanted to know her father. Their mother wouldn't have allowed Paul back into her younger daughter's life unless she was certain he was a good influence. Eve wanted that for Emily.

"I'd like to try." He smiled at her, and she recognized the grin. It was the same one she saw in the mirror. "T'is the season, right?"

"Right."

"Maybe we could start with you coming to my birthday dinner," he suggested. "Saturday night at the Motor Inn Restaurant. I can make the reservation for four. Or five, if there is someone you'd like to bring." He didn't raise his eyebrow at her, or grin, but Eve could tell he was doing it on the inside.

"Four will be fine." Eve wasn't getting into her personal life with her father, especially at their first family dinner in over a decade.

"Thanks, Evie-bear. Evie," he corrected himself immediately. "I'll see you on Saturday. Feel better soon. Do you need me to get you anything? The store is still open for another half hour."

"I'm fine." Eve pointed to the bag on her kitchen counter. "Nick brought over a ton of cold supplies. Thanks anyway."

He didn't hide his grin, and Eve wanted to slap herself upside the head at the slip. She was glad when her dad left without further comment, both because she didn't want to think too hard as to why Nick had been over twice in one day, and because her cold was demanding one more nap before she went to bed for the night.

11. NICK

NICK DIDN'T LIKE WORKING Saturdays, but sometimes it was necessary. Like when it was two weeks 'til Christmas, there were two teams in the warehouses, and North Pole Unlimited had triple the usual number of trucks on the roads making deliveries.

Thankfully, decades of experience and official procedures for every imaginable scenario meant things were moving smoothly. Nick still felt better for checking. He also dropped off two trays of mini cinnamon buns for the shippers and loaders in the warehouse. The eight dozen bite-sized buns from Norma's wouldn't last long, but he wanted the workers to know they were appreciated.

He made a final check of his office. His email was closed. The lights were off. The cabinets were locked. Everyone else was smart enough to be home with their families on the second weekend before Santa came.

He heard the racket first, then spotted the noise-makers as they came around the corner. "Jilly, why are you here?"

"Oh dear, we're busted," she whispered.

"Hi, Nick!"

He groaned. "Hi, Gran. Please tell me you didn't bring a potential date to my office." She'd gone an entire week without offering to make an introduction to a new single friend, and he wanted to keep the streak alive.

"No, not this time." Adelaide ran her hand along the wainscoting in the central office corridor. "It's my first year not being in here for the Christmas rush. I missed it. Jilly said she'd bring me in for a visit before we headed out for coffee." Her eyes focused on the door at the end of the hall. The bottom slide had "President" on it, but the upper one was blank. "North doesn't have a nameplate yet."

"It's on back order," Nick said. "Again. We've had three so far, and they've all had different spelling mistakes. It's become an office joke."

Jilly patted her arm. "I promised Adelaide we'd check out the storerooms. We're using all new holiday stationery designs this year, and I think she'd like some samples."

Nick backed away, hands fending off an invisible danger. "That's it. I'm escaping before the crafting talk starts. Enjoy your coffee date."

"What are you doing this afternoon, my favourite grandchild of the moment?"

Nick was saved by the cell, in more than one way, when he saw the name on the screen. "Excuse me for a minute," he said to his grandmother. "Hi, Eve," he said a little louder than necessary.

He should have felt guilty, but he didn't. Not when he saw the grin on Jilly's face and the nudge she gave Adelaide. "What's up?"

"That's what I was going to ask you. Do you and your awesome truck have any plans today?" Eve asked.

"Generally, when people ask about my truck, they need a favour. A moving favour."

"Then you're already prepared to say yes. Excellent!" she crowed.

At the snicker, he realized the women beside him could hear both sides of his conversation. "What precisely do you need help with?"

"Greenjeans Grocery Coffee Club deliveries."

"I'll be right over."

"I'm at the store. Thanks, Nick."

His grandmother's smile was blinding. "Eve sounds like a good one. I always liked the idea behind the Coffee Club. That's why we sponsored it for the first five years until it could stand on its own."

Nick hadn't realized NPU had participated in the local event, but he wasn't surprised. It was a good idea, and one the community had desperately needed as the company was still growing. "I should get going."

"Say 'hi' to Eve for us," Jilly said.

"You couldn't resist, could you?"

"Nope." His executive assistant spun on her heel. "Come on, Adelaide. You're going to love the card designs this year. They are all baby animals. I don't know where Joy found them."

Nick headed in the other direction before he was subjected to any more craft talk. Knowing his grandmother, she could go all afternoon. Besides, Eve sounded abnormally frazzled.

He parked Clementine behind December's largest grocery store. The rolling doors at the docking bay were open, and a dozen people buzzed around on the crowded cement pad, dropping items in boxes and marking things down on clipboards. A stack of sealed and labelled boxes waited at the edge of the bay.

"Nick, are you here to help?" Clara Dempsey asked. The grocery store owner was a happy, heavy-set woman with ever-changing hair colours. For the season, she had bright green tips peeking out from under a Santa hat.

"Eve called me. Actually, she called for my truck and said I was welcome to come with it," he joked.

"Thank goodness. Three of our drivers are out with colds. We need to get all these orders out today. Can your truck take any of them?" she asked.

Eve stumbled in their direction, her arms filled with boxes. She squatted and let them fall the final few inches to the floor. "You made it. Consider yourself recruited." She pulled a Santa hat from one of the many pockets on her jacket and offered it to him. It matched the one on her head, as well as Clara's.

"Do you buy these things in bulk?" he asked. There had to be half a dozen of them in the storage area.

"They multiply in decoration boxes, and the next year you have twice as many as you packed away. It's a real thing," Eve insisted. "Put it on."

Nick reluctantly pulled it over his head. It flattened his blond hair to his scalp, and the fake white fur trim tickled his ears. "Happy?"

"Ecstatic. Come on up and we'll explain what's going on." Eve offered her hand, and he took it as he hopped onto the elevated platform. She didn't let it go as she dragged him to the first stack of packages. "Like Clara said, we're three drivers down. These packages are all ready to go to the first set of Coffee Club members. We want to have them delivered at least a week before Christmas, which leaves us this weekend because the twenty-fourth is next Monday. You know how it works, right?"

He did. The Greenjeans Coffee Club was based on the old, weekly-subscription model of Christmas hampers. Shoppers registered in January, and they could add a minimum of two dollars—the price of a cup of coffee—to their bill every time they shopped. The store tracked the contributions, and come December, club members had enough to fill a hamper with enough groceries to get them through the Christmas season, leaving funds free for other holiday expenses.

The store added their own loyalty bonuses to top up the hampers with all kinds of goodies. People could track how much they'd paid, but the store assembled the boxes. If some families who could use a little boost received more than others, nobody complained; no one knew how much other families had saved, or what the store's prices were. As Adelaide had mentioned, NPU had donated to the Coffee Club's slush fund for years to make up some of the difference. Now, it was self-sustaining through generous members and other local businesses.

"At least we don't have to worry about keeping them refrigerated," Nick noted. "Can they be frozen?"

"There are some potatoes and carrots in with the canned goods, but they should be okay if we're quick enough," Clara said.

How could he say no to such a good cause? Especially with Eve looking at him like she was. "Okay, let's get Clementine loaded."

Eve gave his arm an excited squeeze. "You heard the

man. Let's get this red sled loaded for Christmas!" she shouted to the other workers.

They quickly shoved and jostled boxes into position, and in minutes, he had eight deliveries loaded and ready to go. Eve hopped into the passenger seat. "I'm your navigator." She fished a baggie out of yet another jacket pocket and set it on Clementine's dashboard. "And snack provider. They're gingerbread...pieces," she said, frowning at the decapitated cookies.

No matter where they went, they were greeted with smiles. With a quick reminder that some of the stuff had to be refrigerated, they wished the recipients a merry Christmas and moved onto the next house. The first eight were all in town. The next batch of six were out in the country, south of December. While he supervised the loading of the truck, Eve disappeared.

She came back with two travel mugs and two massive, unbroken gingerbread men. "To keep our strength up," she told him.

"Yes, because highway driving can be utterly exhausting," he agreed.

"See, you get it." She tapped his cookie with hers. "Cheers to my emergency delivery guy." She promptly bit the cookie's head off. Eve grinned at his shocked look. "What? I'm being as humane as possible," she mumbled as she brushed crumbs from her lips.

Nick hadn't met a woman who made him laugh like her in ages. "Once we get these all dropped off, how many deliveries are left?" They might be able to squeeze one more load in before supper, but it would be a stretch.

"We have another team doing rural drop-offs too. If we can do another four after this load, that'll be forty for the day. We tried to get all the country deliveries scheduled for today. It's easy enough for people with cars to drop off the ones in town." Eve relaxed into the bench seat. "I loved delivery day when I was a kid."

"What did you like best about it?"

"Planning the menu. Mom and Em and I would unpack it on the kitchen table and figure out how many new recipes we could try for side dishes. We always got some weird stuff in our hamper, stuff my mom would never have bought on her own, so it was fun to find canned smoked oysters, or olives, or water crackers. We'd always have a fancy snack supper on Christmas Eve, and save the turkey and new dishes for Christmas."

Nick had volunteered at the Coffee Club when he was home from university on winter breaks. Oysters and olives were never part of the main hamper. They were some of the extras the store provided, usually to families who would consider them a fancy treat.

He'd been lucky, and his family had made sure he'd known it. The pantry was always full, and Christmas dinner was spread across the dining room table, or the kitchen table, or the Ping-Pong table in the basement, depending on whose house they were at and how many cousins were attending. "This is payback?"

"Oh, yeah. I knew Greenjeans was topping up our basket by the time I was fourteen. I could either resent it and ruin Christmas for my sister and embarrass my mother, or I could help out and feel like I earned it. My mom and I volunteered every year. We still do. She's inside right now, helping with the packing."

He needed to thank his parents again. He'd also like to shake Eve's mother's hand if he ever met her.

They made their stops and were back in time to catch a lull at the Pumpkin Patch. This time, he refilled the travel mugs while Eve sorted out a snafu with their next set of deliveries. When he returned, he saw three packages in the back. "Not four?"

"One of the families was in town, so they picked it up themselves."

All told, he put on two hundred miles, over three hundred kilometres, with Eve by the time the sun went down. His back was killing him because of Clementine's old-fashioned seat, but it was worth it.

When they arrived back at Greenjeans, he pulled to the curb and let the engine idle. It hadn't been what he'd intended to do on his Saturday afternoon, but now he wouldn't have spent it any other way. "What's next for you?"

Eve sighed heavily. "I have to get ready for supper with my dad. It's his birthday."

"I didn't get the impression you two were close."

"We're not. We're trying something new for Emily. The tension between us is making things hard on her, and she doesn't deserve that. So, I'm sucking it up, which tonight means supper at the Motor Inn Restaurant." After seeing her natural smile all afternoon, Nick judged the fake one she gave him a three out of ten.

"You're a good sister."

"I really am. How about you?"

"I'm a lousy sister. For a spoiled baby brother, I'm pretty good, though. Both my older brothers would say so."

That earned him a laugh.

"Thanks for everything today," Eve said. "We couldn't have done it without you."

"It was all my pleasure." Nick waited till she was back in her own truck before he headed home. The Christmas lights he had on the window welcomed him; they were on a timer. His furnace was blowing at full blast, but somehow, he couldn't shake his chill. When he took off his coat, a baggie fell out of the pocket. It contained two tiny gingerbread tots. Then it felt a little warmer.

12. EVE

EVE TWISTED her blonde hair into a bun and donned the sleek black blouse she'd received for her birthday two years earlier. She'd already changed into her good jeans and pulled her thin leather dress boots out from the back of her closet and dusted them off. If she were going to do this, she was going to give it her best shot. For Emily.

The Motor Inn Restaurant had garland wound between the banisters that segregated the coat room from the hostess's stand, and red and silver balls hanging from the dining room's four chandeliers. Aside from that, the panelling and brown plaid upholstery were as dark and dismal as ever.

She hadn't bought her father a present but managed to find a silly card in the stack she kept on hand for emergency occasions.

"Thank you," he said after he read it and laughed appropriately.

"You're welcome."

Emily kept the conversation rolling with tales of school and her upcoming solo. She tried to joke about the silliness of a high school still putting on a Christmas concert, but Eve would have none of it.

"It's a legitimate talent show, and you have real talent. I know for a fact they didn't take everyone who auditioned. People are paying to come to hear you sing. Brag about it!" Eve insisted.

"Your mom says you have an excellent voice. I already bought a ticket and I'll be front and centre in the first row," Paul said.

Eve quickly asked which songs she'd be performing. She didn't want her sister taking note of her father's promise. Not until he'd proved himself.

"'Christmas Eve'. The Kelly Clarkson song. We—all the participating seniors—are doing an acapella version of 'Silver Bells,' too."

"'Silver Bells' is one of my favourites," her mother exclaimed.

"I know. You've only been playing it since I was born. I've had the lyrics memorized since I was four," Emily joked.

That led to questions about whether or not Emily had a duet partner, which her sister quickly redirected toward Eve. "Speaking of partners, why didn't you tell me you were seeing Hot Nick?"

"Hot Nick?" Did everybody call him by that nickname?

"Everyone says you're the funniest team at trivia night. Penny said he came with you on"—Emily cut herself off, looking around the room to ensure she wouldn't be overheard—"the Bucky sighting." She stared at Eve over the top of her water glass.

"We're not dating. We were at the pub playing trivia when I got the call. He offered to come with me. That's all." She was still hung up on people referring to him as Hot Nick.

"The trivia part was the date, not the dog-chasing. Got it."

Emily could be such a brat. "Not a date," Eve growled.

Eve had no idea why her father decided to join forces against her. "I was grocery shopping this afternoon. Clara said that you two teamed up today, as well."

"We needed a truck!" she protested.

"Was he the only person in town you could call?"

"At last minute? Yes. I—we—were lucky he agreed to help. We delivered hampers for six hours. That's not a date. That's almost a full workday."

"So you invited him to your father's birthday supper in compensation?" her mom asked.

"What? No!" Eve would be lucky if Nick answered the phone if she called him in the next week after everything she'd put him through today.

But there he was, in a brown-and-blue knit sweater with a dress shirt underneath. He was in dress slacks, too, and leather loafers. She'd never seen him dressed up before, and for the first time, she understood his nickname.

Eve recognized the lady on his arm, too. It was his grandmother, who was equally done up. She expected a nod. A wave at best. Instead, the pair walked directly to their table. "Happy birthday, Paul," Adelaide Klassen said in greeting.

"Thank you. You, too," her father said.

Twin birthday celebrations made better sense than Nick just happening by on chance. It was still a strange coincidence.

"Would you like to join us for dessert?" Paul continued.

Eve bit her lip rather than shouting "No!" like she wanted to. Her dad could invite whoever he wanted to his birthday party.

Nick helped their waiter shift two chairs to the ends of their table. Adelaide sat by Paul; Nick took the seat beside her. Eve kicked her sister under the table in an effort to get Emily to wipe the smile off her face.

It didn't work.

"It's your birthday, too?" Eve asked Adelaide, in case she'd misunderstood.

"Next week," the other woman confirmed. "I asked Nick to take me out for birthday cake tonight. I wasn't going to miss a chance to have the cocoa-mocha ice-cream pie here."

"That's what we all ordered," Eve said. It was one thing about the dining room she'd never change.

"It was my last chance for it, since I know work will get worse before it gets better until the twenty-fifth. If he's lucky, he'll be able to take a night off for another Bucky search. Unless they catch that ninja dog."

"Have you heard something?" Emily perked up in her seat. She was usually quiet around strangers, but Adelaide had hit upon a topic guaranteed to draw her out.

Her mom tugged Emily's blonde ponytail. "Exactly how many people did you rope into searching for Bucky?"

Emily shrugged before she grinned at Adelaide. "I might have contacted North Pole Unlimited's Community Participation department and asked if they could put the word out to local employees. It was a community service!"

Adelaide laughed. "It wasn't quite what we had in

mind when we created the department, but it fit within the mandate. And to answer your question, yes, I got an update before Nick picked me up. I'm friends with the Shaws, who own the property next to the Georges. They gave Operation Retriever permission to do what was necessary to try to catch Bucky. They almost had him this afternoon, but that dog is wily. He got away, but now they have absolute confirmation he's staying in the area."

Emily danced in her seat in glee. Eve reached across the table and gave her a high five. "Yes," Eve said, answering her sister's unanswered question. "I'll go out again when I'm not working and look for him."

"How about you, Nick? Will you help?" Emily asked.

She'd been such a good baby sister. Eve was going to miss Emily...after she killed her.

"I'll make myself available. Eve knows what I charge," he promised. He shot Eve a smile she didn't understand until he added, "Heads attached."

She burst into laughter. Perhaps the rest of the night wouldn't be a complete disaster.

13. NICK

NICK WAS FEELING GENEROUS, so he stopped at the IT department and at Logistics to share his donut bounty. He still had three left, including a raspberry jelly donut. Nick couldn't believe they'd ignored the jelly. Once they'd made their selections, he informed the remaining staff they had until they'd finished their donuts or until eleven o'clock to clear out. It was December twenty-fourth, and everybody had more important places to be than in their cubicle answering emails that could wait till after Christmas.

Except him.

His jaw stretched so wide when he yawned he could have stuffed a whole donut in his mouth. He should have; he needed the sugar rush. All he had to do was stay awake for a few more hours until he could go home and nap in front of the television while an endless loop of an anonymous flannel-covered arm dropping a log on the crackling fire played on the Fireside Channel.

It had been nonstop since he'd arrived the previous Monday morning. Last week had been the final full work week before Christmas, and all through the company, Nick had been tracking down missing timesheets, confirming flights for truckers who were dropping their loads at destinations that were not close to home, and putting out fires of all other flavours, since over half of NPU's managers were already on vacation.

He hadn't even been able to go to trivia night. He'd tried, but it had been eight o'clock before he'd gotten out the door. Nick had arrived at Garland's Pub to hear that Eve had arrived at seven and waited half an hour before getting called out. Nick stuck it out anyway, on the off chance she'd return. He managed to get an order in to the kitchen before it closed for a night, and he decided not to waste the opportunity.

He texted Eve the trivia questions as they appeared on the screen.

She texted her answers back. It was obvious she wasn't cheating and using Google.

The largest shark was not the Great White.

Jack the Ripper did not find his victims in White Castle.

The world's longest marathon was not five hundred miles and then five hundred more, and participants did not fall down at the organizer's door when they were finished. Nick couldn't breathe for laughing. When he showed the screen to Mikki, she read it aloud to the other players. They gave Team Awesome Truck zero points for their answer, but they were on the board. At the bottom.

In the final hour of the game, they earned two points. There'd been applause when they got them.

The next day, Eve texted him a question about Olympic hockey and the answer. He'd responded with a fact about British royalty. Their exchanges continued all week, interspersed with notifications of the daily soup from Norma's Buns and dessert special from the Pumpkin Patch.

There was no trivia tonight. Eve would be with her family. Nick would be with his.

As soon as he finished.

He'd cleared every problem east of Thunder Bay, allowing those in earlier time zones to start their holidays with a clean slate. He was combining all his notes from northwestern Ontario and Manitoba into one pile when his office door swung inward.

"Nick! What are you doing here?" Jilly held her hand to her chest.

"I work here. Why are you sneaking into my office when your last day of work for the year was Friday?" he asked.

She ran her hand through her hair, turning it into brown spikes. "You aren't supposed to be here."

"It's my office," he repeated. Nick took a second look at his assistant. "Why are you carrying a stepladder?" It was the foldable, two-step one from the storage room.

"Fine!" Jilly stomped across the room and stopped beside the built-in credenza behind his desk. "Go ahead, ruin next Christmas for my son." She flipped the ladder open, climbed it, and stepped onto the top of the cabinet. Her foot nudged his coffeemaker. The pot slid off the element and teetered on the edge before righting itself. "Sorry about that."

Now he knew what had happened to his last one. "What are you doing?"

She squared her feet to balance herself. Once she was steady, she stretched and pushed aside a ceiling tile.

"Jilly!"

Then she began pulling things out of the ceiling. Rolls of wrapping paper. Shipping boxes. Store bags with their handles tied shut. A tin of what Nick recognized as very expensive, imported shortbread from England.

"This was the perfect hiding place. Dan doesn't have access. George never knew about it, and you didn't catch on last year. But now you know, which means my son will worm it out of you before next year. Now I have to find a new spot." She climbed down and arranged all her squirrelled away items on the edge of his desk.

"Are you saying you've been hiding your son's Christmas presents in your boss's office? For years?"

Her stare was chilling. "I *was*. Do you know how hard it is to keep secrets when your only beloved child is ninety percent bloodhound? That boy can sniff out a present at one hundred yards. In fact, he's done it, which is why I couldn't hide his gifts at the neighbours after he turned nine. This was the perfect place, and now you ruined it!"

"It's *my* office."

"Which was why it was perfect." With an ease Nick had yet to master, Jilly spread some paper on the clear countertop and plopped a box on top of it. She whipped a pair of scissors out of her back pocket, zipped the blade along the edge of the roll, and began folding it around the box before Nick would have made the first snip.

She smacked three stickers on the sides and bottom and moved onto the next gift. All four packages were wrapped and beribboned in five minutes. "Done."

"Why aren't you in shipping?" Nick asked.

"That's where I started with NPU." She put the remnants of her gift wrapping in an empty store bag and flexed her arms. "I still hold the department record for most gifts wrapped in an hour, and for fastest wrap of a hexagon box."

Now that she'd stopped worrying about her son finding his unwrapped gifts, Jilly helped herself to a cup of coffee. "What are you doing here at noon on the twenty-fourth, boss?"

"Making sure everyone gets home for Christmas. I have a dozen more things to check, then I'm out of here." He figured he had about three more hours to go before two and half days of utter slothfulness.

"What are you doing for the holidays?"

Nick's eyes narrowed. Jilly knew this. They'd discussed it in detail on Friday. "We're doing the big family thing tomorrow. Why?"

"I was wondering what Eve was up to."

"I imagine she's spending Christmas with her own family if she's not working." Nick didn't know if Eve's father would be included in the celebration. With what she'd said about Paul LeBlanc, Nick leaned toward no.

Jilly nodded again. "If you're serious about that girl, you need to stop keeping her to yourself. She should meet your family."

He ignored the phone ringing on his desk. Eve should meet his family? "Excuse me?"

"You should invite her over for the Klassen Christmas Open House."

He choked on air. Anyone and everyone in town was welcome at the open house. *Bringing* somebody was an entirely different situation. For Jilly to suggest such a thing was completely inappropriate. "I've known Eve for less than a month. We're not serious enough for that."

Jilly grinned. He took a minute to replay his last sentence. "We aren't serious at all," he said again, too late.

The damage was done. Nick thought he'd teased and inferred just enough to stop his grandmother and her accomplices from concocting unwelcome set-ups and introductions for a while. Her thinking they were dating casually was fine. Thinking they were in a relationship was a step too far.

"I think you were right the first time. Adelaide agrees with me. She's quite upset that she's only had two quick introductions, and both of those in a professional capacity. She thinks you ought to have invited Eve, so she's decided to take the task upon herself."

Nick expected white, blinding panic to swamp him at the words. Instead, he felt nothing. A minute later, he realized he was in shock. "What did she do?"

14. EVE

WHEN HER ALARM went off at six, the first words she heard were the weather report. Eve took one look out the window and wished she could stay under the covers. After a full week of never-ending overcast skies, the storm swirling around the Great Lakes had decided to head their way. The radio reported it was crawling over northeastern Minnesota, dumping inches of snow in its path on a direct course to southeast Manitoba.

Eve groaned as she rolled out of bed. Each storm was unique, but the chaos they caused was always the same. She was about to get swamped with calls. Mother Nature didn't care if it was the day before Christmas.

She turned up the radio while she was in the shower. Highway 75 turned into Highway 29 at the American border and ran from Winnipeg to Kansas City. At the moment, the announcers said everything north of the border was still open, but Eve didn't expect it to stay that way much longer. The wind would white-out the area as it shifted snow from one field to another, making visibility worse by the hour.

Her first call came in at six thirty, while she was smearing a thick layer of strawberry jelly over her peanut butter toast. Without looking at her phone, Eve made a bet with herself that the emergency was a dead battery.

She was right. In fact, she won two of the four battery bets she made before she pulled up behind a heavy work truck with a cap on the back. This time, she knew she was wrong before she made it to the driver. A puddle of fluid leaking from under the chassis was a dead giveaway the problem couldn't be solved with a jumpstart.

The woman who climbed out of the cab to greet her looked familiar, although Eve didn't immediately place her. Her client did. "Hello, again. Eve, right?"

"Hi."

The other woman laughed. "You must meet a ton of people. I'm Laurel Murphy. We met in the parking lot at the craft show a couple weeks back. You were helping Nick Klassen with his truck. I drove his grandmother home."

"Right." Now Eve remembered. This was the woman Nick's grandmother was trying to set him up with.

"Sorry about that, by the way. If I'd known Nick was seeing somebody, I wouldn't have agreed to the invitation."

"We aren't dating." Why did everyone think they were dating?

"Anyway, it worked out great for me. Adelaide introduced me to another grandson." Laurel's eyes twinkled, and Eve laughed when she raised her eyebrows. "Those Klassen boys are something else."

"I'll take your word for it."

"You should find out for yourself."

"I'll consider it," Eve said politely. It wasn't Laurel's

fault she had the wrong impression, so arguing with her wouldn't solve anything. Eve knelt on the snow-crusted gravel road and peered under the chassis. "Did you roll to a stop?" she asked.

"Pretty much. A yellow dog popped out of the ditch and darted across the road in front of me. I was standing on the brakes before they kicked in. Please don't say I need new brakes."

Eve's news would be a nasty addition to an already expensive month, but it couldn't be helped. "Sorry. You need new brakes. Merry Christmas. Where do you want me to take you?"

A couple of calls later, Laurel arranged to have her sister meet her at the garage near Brunkild and get the rest of the way home.

Her next was in town. "George, we have to stop meeting like this." They'd met at the hood of his car twice already since September. It was starting to be a habit. "I thought we discussed you buying a new battery. Two weeks ago," Eve emphasised.

"I'm getting one for Christmas when I'm in the city. We're already packed. Once we're started, Louise and I will be on our way. If we get there."

"We'll get you there," Eve promised. "Then you can start the celebrations."

"How about you?" The senior pulled his toque lower on his head as a particularly hard wind gust rocked them both.

"As soon as I'm done here, I'm off to the Christmas concert at the high school. Emily's singing." Eve had heard "Silver Bells" a dozen times over the last week, and it sounded better every time.

"What about tomorrow? The only downside about

having Christmas in the city at our son's house is that we miss the Klassens' open house."

Eve frowned. "Tomorrow, I'm on call. I hope to have hot turkey and stuffing and gravy and cranberry sauce. Worst case scenario is that I'll have it as leftovers."

"Stuffing and gravy and cranberry sauce? All together?"

"Is there any other way?" She waved her hand to indicate he should get behind the wheel.

The senior laughed. "Yes. Generally, it's just one."

"Amateurs," Eve joked.

After the engines whined and growled for a bit, George's car finally started. "Do you have gas? If you turn it off to fill the tank, I can't guarantee it'll start again," Eve warned him.

"We're good. Thank you. Don't go filling up on turkey. Save some room for the spread at the Klassens'. I promise it'll be worth it. They do a honey ham that melts in your mouth."

Eve looked at George in confusion. "I'm not going to the open house."

Now he looked confused. "Adelaide said Nick was bringing you to introduce you to the family."

"We aren't dating!" Why did she have to keep telling people that?

"That's not what Adelaide says," George insisted. He laughed when she growled at him and said good-bye.

Her dispatcher took pity on her, and she made it all the way to her next destination without a single emergency. Then she logged out for the three-hour break she'd requested.

Eve pulled her wrecker into the high school parking lot as the numbers on her dashboard clock hit six. She didn't have time to go home to change, but her mother had promised her dinner-to-go while they waited for the concert to start at six-thirty before she was back on duty. It meant she'd be on call all night till two in the morning on Christmas Day and go back on at two in the afternoon. The timing was doubly horrible, both for the holiday and because she'd be on for the brunt of the storm as it moved in, but she happily took the bad shift for the chance to hear her sister sing her mom's favourite Christmas carol.

The parking lot was full and recently cleared of snow. Eve had passed a handful of plows on the street, trying to keep up with the snowfall. She parked near the exit and tromped through fresh flakes that covered the toes of her boots.

Her mother saved her a seat on the aisle. The chair on the other side was empty. "Where's Dad?" Eve asked as she unwound her red-and-white striped scarf.

Helen's lips pressed together in a tight line. "I sent him a text. He still has time."

But she didn't expect him to get there. Not in time to hear Emily sing. Her tone said she didn't expect him at all. Eve's stomach churned. "Does Emily know?"

Her mom shook her head. "I tried to tell her not to get her hopes up."

"Men suck." Eve flopped into her chair and grabbed gratefully at the insulated container her mother passed her.

"All men?"

"So far." She peeled back the lid. "Moms, however, are wonderful, amazing creatures of perfection. Thank you." The cheesy, beefy, tomato sauce that stuck to the baked rigatoni was solid enough not to drip as she attacked the first real food she'd had in hours.

"Which men?" her mother pressed. "Besides your father."

"Nobody. Definitely nobody named Nick Klassen, that's for sure."

"Hot Nick?"

"Don't you start!"

Her mother laughed. "I'm just teasing. Although having met him, I get the nickname. I thought you two weren't dating."

"Me, too, but according to his grandmother and everyone she's spoken to, I'm mistaken."

Eve finished the pasta and tucked the container of cookies into her jacket pocket for later. The lights flashed on and off, and the conversations surrounding them died down as the emcee took centre stage to start the show.

15. NICK

NICK DIDN'T GET AWAY AS EARLY as he'd hoped, but eventually, he made it to the bottom of his to-do list. Then he got a call and added one more thing to it.

His grandmother had phoned him just as he was leaving the office. "Nick, Noel is down with a stomach bug. I hate to call at the last minute, but can you take me to North's?" she'd asked.

He hadn't needed to hear more. "I'll leave now." The normally fifteen-minute trip from the office took closer to thirty, and Clementine threw a fit as he turned onto the lane to the family homestead. She shuddered and rocked, and he fought to keep her on the narrow gravel road until he was parked in front of the house. The snow brushed the rims of his winter tires, except on the front passenger side where it encroached on the hubcap. He looked at the listing vehicle in disappointment. "Really?" he asked the old girl.

His gran was waiting at the front door, an overnight bag at her feet. "Are the roads that bad? Are we going to make it to December?"

"Not in Clementine," he growled.

"Come inside and let's figure this out."

Nick heard her flicking switches as she moved through the living room. The table lamps sprung to life, and the Christmas tree in the corner went from a dark mass to a beacon of light. "How have you not blown a fuse with all these decorations plugged in?" he asked.

Adelaide gave him a disappointed look. "We had the place rewired with all of this in mind." She tossed a pillow nestled into the brown recliner onto the sofa and sat on the edge of the seat, rocking it slightly. "Do you want to take my car?"

He hated to leave Clementine alone and broken, but it was the safest bet. She'd be fine here until someone could come out and look at her. "Yes."

It was a good thing they weren't playing poker, because their best bet was a bust. Adelaide's SUV was just as dead as his vehicle. "I guess we're calling North. Or we could call your lovely girlfriend. I would love to see her come riding to your rescue," his grandmother teased.

Right, his girlfriend, the tow truck driver. "Eve is at the concert tonight. Her sister is singing." He hadn't memorized Eve's schedule; Emily had mentioned it at dinner the previous weekend.

Adelaide rubbed her forehead. "Right, I knew that. North and Alicia would have left for it already, too. I guess we'll have to wait for the concert to end."

Nick knew his mom's childhood house as well as his own. He eased into the kitchen and filled the kettle. "Peppermint or chamomile?"

"Chamomile, please."

She might live alone, but his grandmother's fridge was stuffed to overflowing, mostly with things for the buffet table the next day. Nick lifted some of the tinfoil coverings, trying to muffle the sounds.

"Nick, you stay out of those. They're for tomorrow."

"We're stranded in a snowstorm and need supper," he shouted back to the living room.

There was a pause. "No more than one of anything for each of us. Jiggle the platters around so there isn't a gap to show what we took," she ordered.

Nick grinned at the fridge. He already knew that trick.

He quickly fixed two plates and returned to the living room. Despite the wind howling outside, he didn't light the fire, not without being able to take a look at the roof to ensure the chimney was clear. Instead, he dropped a throw pillow over his gran's lap and brought her a cup of tea. "You are such a good boy. And Eve is such a sweet girl. Pretty. Funny. Everyone says she makes you laugh. She's a good fit for you," she said as she patted his cheek.

Things had definitely gone too far. "You have the wrong idea about me and Eve."

"What? She's not a sweet girl?" she demanded. "Excuse me, but didn't she ask you to help her with the Coffee Club? Weren't you right beside her when she went out looking for little Madison Hill's missing dog? Why, Eve is all heart."

"I know that, Gran. I meant—"

"Isn't she pretty enough for you?"

That definitely wasn't the problem. Nick always considered himself an equal-opportunity dater, but now he knew he preferred brown-eyed blondes. "No, Eve is very pretty," And funny, too," he added to cut off her next argument. She'd proved that with her texts, although he had noticed the lack of them during the day today. He figured the oncoming storm had kept her hopping. He'd barely made it to the homestead in his truck; he hated to think of what the snow would do to little cars on the highway.

"Then why aren't you interested?"

"I don't have time to be interested." It was an old refrain, and a true one, but this was the first time even he was tired of it. Or maybe he was just tired.

"Women like her don't rescue you from the side of the road every day, Nick."

"I know." He did. None of his grandmother's matchmaking attempts had come close to Eve. He was sure they were all sweet and pretty and funny, but Eve was the only one who made the combination work for him.

"Finally. What are you going to do about it?" she asked.

"At eight in the evening on December twenty-fourth? Nothing. I'll call her tomorrow and wish her a Merry Christmas." Nick crossed the living room and crouched in front of the recliner. "What I will not be doing is inviting her to the family's open house. I met Eve a month ago. Blindsiding her with something like that isn't fair. Do you understand?"

His gran met his eyes. "I understand perfectly. You will not be inviting Eve to the open house tomorrow."

"Good."

The grandfather clock in the corner chimed eight. "I suppose we should call North and ask if she can come get us."

Nick shook his head. "She can take just you. I'll call Eve. I've decided I don't want to leave Clementine stranded here. We shouldn't have two dead vehicles between the two of us."

His text to Eve went unanswered. His call went directly to voicemail. His third call, to the motor league, confirmed calls were stacking up with the arriving storm. Since he was safe at a residence, his call had low priority. He was in for a long wait.

"It's fine, I can crash on the sofa," Nick repeated. His cousin had arrived an hour after Adelaide's call, crawling up the driveway in a heavy-duty SUV they should have heard coming. "If I'm still snowed in by morning, you know where to send the rescue party," Nick assured her.

"Don't eat all my cookies. You'll make yourself sick," Adelaide warned as she carefully zipped her jacket over the tails of her scarf. They'd already transferred the rest of the food to the trunk.

"I won't."

"There are more chocolate drops in the freezer," she said a second later.

"That knowledge does not help my self-control."

"You can gorge a little bit."

"Call me when you get to North's, so I know you made it okay."

Nick got a text from the motor league at nine thirty. He could expect a two-to-four hour wait. The next update changed it to four-to-six hours. The clock was ticking toward eleven when headlights coming up the driveway shone through the living room window and illuminated the far wall.

16. EVE

EVE WAS cold and tired and still had five hours to go. She'd come out of the concert to see that the brunt of the storm had moved on to Saskatchewan to blow itself out. The RCMP hadn't closed the roads, but that didn't mean people could drive willy-nilly through the remnants blowing across the highway.

Although they tried.

She also had another call waiting. That made three people she'd pulled out of the ditch in one day. Thankfully, none of them involved injuries.

She wasn't done. Her dispatcher sent her another name.

With all the Klassens in the area, she couldn't be certain this Nick was her Nick. Her trivia partner Nick, not *her* Nick. Eve didn't know the address, but it was close to his grandmother's home. She scrolled through past messages and realized he'd texted her while she was at Emily's concert.

He hadn't been the only one.

"*Hi, Eve. This is Adelaide Klassen. Nick's truck is*

dead at my place. I hope you can help him. We both think you're wonderful. Thanks."

She kept scrolling.

Eve didn't know how Adelaide had gotten her number, but she'd made good use of it. At nine, Eve received another one. *Nick can bring you to our open house at North's tomorrow unless you are on call and need to drive yourself. The rest of the family is looking forward to meeting you."* Her next text contained the address.

Obviously, the nice old lady had got her wires crossed. Nick hadn't invited Eve anywhere, and she definitely wasn't meeting his family.

Her phone pinged again.

"Nick didn't tell me your favourite desserts. Let me know. North's kitchen is fully stocked."

A little later. *"Nick says you're still working and haven't made it to the house yet. Such a long workday on Christmas Eve. The open house runs all afternoon, so you can sleep in and come later. Nick will pick you up whenever you want."*

"What on earth is going on?" she asked herself. What had Nick been saying about her?

A text from a new number. *"This is North, Nick's cousin. Adelaide says Nick says gingerbread and shortbread and we have both. I'll save some for you because my family all have hollow legs. Looking forward to meeting Nick's new girlfriend after all the stories."*

It was official. The Klassen clan was crazy. She'd get him back on the road and head in the other direction. Nobody invited their game night partner to a family event, especially a major occasion. Either Nick's entire family was trivia nuts of the highest order eager to induct a new member into their cult...

Or Nick had plans for her that he hadn't bothered to share.

That annoyed her. She liked him. She liked the odd-facts texting thing they had going on. She liked driving around with him; he was fun and good company. His looks didn't hurt, either. She was looking forward to their next trivia night, and he'd indicated he was, too.

But he hadn't said anything beyond that.

Eve turned off the highway onto a country road that hadn't been ploughed. A double furrow ran down the centre of it, left by brave travellers who'd passed since the storm had ended.

There were no streetlights in the country, and tonight, there was neither moon nor stars. They'd all been blotted out by the clouds. Her headlights spanned both lanes, lighting up the blowing snow until it looked like she was entering hyperspace and each flake was a star speeding past.

The turn-off to Adelaide's house was pristine but for a single set of tracks. She lumbered down the driveway and saw Nick's truck parked in front. Footprints and lumps of snow circled his recently brushed-off, shiny red classic. One problem was immediately apparent. Poor Clementine had a limp.

He met her on the porch, his khaki jacket unzipped, exposing the thick sweater underneath. "I was starting to wonder if you'd forgotten about me."

"How could I forget?" she asked. His family had texted her every hour. "What's the problem, sweetie?"

His voice shot up an octave. "Sweetie?"

"Do you prefer Honeybunch?" Eve asked. "I'm not calling you Pookie."

"Why are you calling me anything? I think you've

been on the road too long." Nick held out a gingerbread man wrapped in a napkin. "You must have low blood sugar."

He seemed thoroughly confused. Eve took it as a good sign. Maybe only his family was nuts. "Thank you. Okay, Nick, what's the problem here?"

"Besides your low blood sugar? And the tire? Her headlights started to flicker just as I turned onto the driveway, which was about the same time as I almost lost control. It all happened at once. Can you take a look?" he asked.

The road under the snow had been full of deep ruts. They might have jogged something loose. "Sure. I'll start with the tire."

It had blown, badly. Fortunately for Nick, the rim looked okay. They heaved the damaged tire into the back of his truck, and Eve carried the replacement over from hers. She normally would have rolled it but pushing it through the snow would take even more energy than carrying it.

The icy bolts burned her fingers, even through her gloves. She dropped more than one nut but eventually got the new tire on. "Would you pop the hood for me, please?" She jammed her hands into her pockets, trying to give them an extra minute to thaw before she had to expose them again.

Nick did as she asked. He'd done a good job parking; the lights from the house shone directly onto the engine. "What do you think?" he asked.

Her phone pinged again. "*Did Nick tell you about the games room? Be warned—we split up the couples. You can be on my team if you're good at darts. I already have a trivia expert.*" Eve couldn't believe his grandmother. Not just for the couple comments, but for banning her from trivia when she didn't even know her.

"A ring would be a good start," Eve said, finally answering his question.

"Are you kidding me? I have to replace Clementine's piston rings?" His voice turned from whiny to confused. "Gordon didn't say a word when he fixed her last time. How can you tell? I haven't even started her for you yet."

"Not for Clementine. You need to give *me* a ring. Being as your grandmother seems to think we're pretty much engaged already!" A hunk of overhanging snow fell off the eavestrough at her shout.

"We're what?" Unlike hers, his voice was level and contained and frighteningly calm.

"Almost affianced? Pre-pre-engaged? Come on, Nick, she told me and everybody else I was your date to your family Christmas party. When was I going to find out?"

17. NICK

WAS GRANDMA-CIDE A THING? Because he was totally going to kill his gran, no matter how good her shortbread was. Especially as he scrolled through the thread on Eve's phone. She'd thrust it at him to prove her argument. "Umm..."

"Did you tell Adelaide I was your date? What have you been saying about me?" Eve demanded.

She was annoyed. He shouldn't find her sparking brown eyes so cute. "Nothing." He also shouldn't lie to her. "Mostly nothing. I might have mentioned you a few times. It's not my fault my grandmother got the wrong impression."

It was funny, though, how he had managed to meet Eve's eyes when she'd spoken, but not when he gave his rebuttal. "Not your fault? It just happened by itself?" Vapour puffed out with her words, giving the impression she was breathing smoke.

"Not exactly." Eve frowned at his non-explanation, and Nick didn't blame her. She deserved more. "My gran has been introducing me to every single woman in the province. When I met you, I didn't have to worry about offending you or letting you down easy because we were strangers. Then I stopped worrying altogether because we had fun. As long as we were having a good time, I didn't want to have to fend off any more of Gran's matchmaking attempts. Telling her we were having fun ensured it."

He hoped Eve understood. He didn't want the roll they were on to end with a big crash because his grandmother had stuck her nose where it didn't belong.

"I had a good time, too, but I don't see how that ended up with her inviting me to your family Christmas, Nick."

"She invited you because she thought I was taking too long." He took a deep breath. This was the hard part. As embarrassing as it was, the truth was better than another lie. "She was right."

He was messing with a good thing. He'd be an idiot to let Eve slip through his fingers. She was all he said he was looking for, and even better, everything he hadn't even known he wanted. "Would you like to come to the Klassen open house with me tomorrow? As my date?" he asked.

"Was that so hard? Yes." Eve grinned at him. "I'm back on call at two in the afternoon, but I would love to go to the open house with you."

He couldn't stop smiling, even when he felt his cheeks burn with cold. "Good. Great!"

"Yes, great." She smiled back at him. Until a gush of wind flew a flurry of flakes into their faces, breaking the mood.

"Can you get me back on the road, so you can get back on the road, so we can both get home, so we can get together tomorrow?" Nick requested. Now that he had a date, he had plans to make, not to mention strategies to concoct to keep his grandmother and the rest of his family from scaring Eve off the first time she officially met them.

"Yes, let's get out of here." She leaned over his truck and grunted. "I don't believe it."

"Please tell me it's not the rings for real."

"It's not. Your battery cables are almost disconnected again. They're barely hanging on." She fiddled with them for a minute, then stood straight. "I think that's it. Why don't you try to start her? If you can get her running, you can lock up Adelaide's house and we can be on our way." She dipped her face to bury her nose in her scarf.

He zipped his jacket and did the same. He was freezing after five minutes. Eve had been in this cold all day. He should have had hot chocolate waiting for her.

Clementine started on the first try, like she'd been waiting for Eve to come along. He darted back to the house, turned off all the lights, and locked it with his key.

"I'll follow you back to December," he said.

"Actually, I wasn't headed home."

"Do you have another call?"

She checked her phone. "No, that's still clear. I was going to swing by Penny George's and the Shaw place. A woman saw a dog run across the road near there earlier today. The description matched Bucky. I want to give it one more shot. We might get lucky," she said.

"It's no problem. Let's go that way." This night of all nights was one to be lucky.

18. EVE

THIRTY MINUTES of slow progress eventually got them to the road leading to Penny George's kennel. A pair of snow-covered hollows guided them down the centre of the road. They weren't fresh, which would have indicated someone driving on them since the snow ended; falling snow would have filled them if they'd been made earlier in the day.

Eve rolled up the lane, leaving Nick on the highway. There was no reason for both of them to risk getting stuck. She knew something was wrong before she arrived.

All the house lights were off. The place was dark except for a couple exterior floodlights set to come on at dusk. "Shoot," Eve said, knowing the phone's speaker would pick it up, "I forgot. Penny isn't boarding over Christmas this year. She took her family south to meet the mouse for the holidays." The yard looked unnaturally still. The snow in the dog run was pristine. From her vantage point by the triple garage, she could even see behind it. No Bucky-type prints marred the white blanket behind the fence either. "I'm not seeing any sign of Bucky," she reported.

"We knew it was a long shot," Nick said.

Eve turned her wrecker around. "I was wishing, though." It wasn't fair. They knew Bucky was in the area. He was *right there*. She and Nick just needed a little help.

"I know. Did you want to get out and look?"

"No." Part of her did, but it was closing in on midnight on Christmas Eve. Common sense had to prevail. "Let's go home."

They had to pass the old Shaw place on the way back to December. Eve wouldn't have looked twice, except for the light shining through what should be the living room window. She slammed on the brakes.

"Eve?"

"Do you see that?" she asked.

"A miniature sleigh and eight tiny reindeer?"

She didn't need him to be funny *now*. "No, the light in the supposedly abandoned house."

"That pooch is smart, but he can't rewire a house," Nick said.

"Exactly. Somebody is in there." With no traffic on the road, she made a wide turn into the lane. Her headlights shone over everything, including the outline of a snow-covered vehicle half in the ditch. "Nick!"

"I see it," he said. "Let's check it out."

The clouds parted for a brief minute, and Eve saw smoke coming from the chimney. "Someone made a fire," she said.

"Dangerous, but better than freezing to death." Nick gestured at the porch. "Do we knock?"

She shook her head. He climbed the rickety stairs first

and pushed the front door open. It squeaked on its hinges. The first thing they saw was a hunched figure throwing a broken balustrade from the front porch into the flames sputtering in the fireplace. The tiny fire had lessened the chill in the air, but it hadn't dismissed it entirely.

Eve's jaw dropped when the figure turned around. "Dad?"

"Hi, Evie-bear, am I glad to see you. Hi, Nick."

"How? Why?" When Paul hadn't been at the concert, she'd assumed he'd left town, or was at a party, or had some other inexcusable excuse for his absence. Being stranded in a snowstorm hadn't made the list. "What are you doing here?"

"I'm stuck."

She should have recognized the ditched car. "Evidently. But why are you *here*?" There was nothing in the area. Aside from the kennel, there weren't any inhabited homes for miles, no friends he could be visiting. It was off the main highway, so it wasn't like he was on his way to the city.

Paul pointed to an armchair Eve hadn't paid any attention to. Sitting on the dust cover was a very familiar, golden retriever. "Bucky!" she shouted.

The dog's tail waved a couple times, but the animal didn't jump up to greet her.

"The old boy's still cold. He wasn't doing great before the fire, but I haven't been able to get it big enough to generate enough heat to warm the room because I have no idea what shape the flue is in."

He hadn't simply bailed on his plans with Emily. He'd missed the concert, but it had been a genuine accident. Emily would be so happy. Eve knew she was.

Thank goodness for Nick. She was too shocked to come up with a plan. He took it all in stride. "Let's douse the fire and get you both out of here. I have my truck, and Eve has hers. We have enough room for both of you." He picked an old metal firewood tray from the floor. "I'll go get some snow to put it out." Nick paused at the door and leveled his blue eyes on her. "I think you wished Madison's Christmas present into existence."

Eve helped her father pull a stack of wood from its place next to the fireplace where it had been drying. "Dad, I don't understand. Why do you have Bucky?"

"I know how hard you and Em have been working to find that mutt. Emily has been talking nonstop about how Bucky has been avoiding the search parties. I wanted to give it another try for her. I figured finding the dog would be better than any present I could buy her, so I came out here this afternoon."

"In the middle of a snowstorm?" she interrupted.

He chuckled, and it turned into a cough. "I still haven't overcome my stubborn streak. I wanted to get my little girl that dog for Christmas. I got it, alright. He was waiting for me on the porch. I saw him from the road. In my hurry to get to the house, I parked my car in a ditch and broke my phone in the process. There was no place around to go for help, so I dug in here. I figured I could try again in the daylight."

"That is both wonderful and stupid," Eve said. "I mean, thank you for finding Bucky. That's terrific, and Em will love it. Unfortunately, as far as she knows, you stood her up at her Christmas concert. She was devastated."

Her father nodded. "I know. I'll fix it, if I survive your mother's attempt to kill me before I can explain."

"I think they'll forgive you quickly once they find out what happened." Eve knew they would.

Nick returned with a tray of snowballs. He gently rolled one into the centre of the flames. The fire flared before it began to fade and sizzle. Two snowballs later, all the flames were out, and a thick layer of ash and water lay at the bottom of the hearth. "That's safe now. Let's hit the road. I think it may start snowing again. Paul, we need to leave your car here tonight."

"No problem," her father quickly agreed.

"How are we going to do this?" Nick asked.

"I have an idea," Eve said.

Nick, Paul, and Bucky piled into his cab. The dog sat on her father's lap. She gave Nick directions and told him where to meet her.

She climbed into her own truck and ordered her phone to call her mom. "Hi, Mom, it's Eve. I'm fine."

A sleepy voice replied, "Merry Christmas, baby. If you're fine, why are you calling so late?"

"Mom, I need you and Emily to get up and get dressed and to meet us on Atkins Road, a block from the Hill's house."

Eve heard her mother yawn. "Your sister's sleeping. Can't this wait till morning?"

"No. Santa will be delivering Bucky to Madison Hill at midnight. I think Emily ought to be there."

There was a pause at the other end of the line. "Emily LeBlanc, get dressed this instant! Santa's coming!" her mom yelled.

The pair were waiting when Eve, Nick, Paul, and Bucky arrived. The three vehicles idled in a row at the cross street to Atkins Road. Eve huddled by Nick's window; Helen and Emily stood sheltered from the wind beside Paul's. "What's the plan, partner?" Nick asked.

"First, we're going to rig some kind of leash for Bucky. Next, you, Emily and I are going to sneak up to the Hill house. We're going to tie him to the railing on the steps. Emily, once we've secured him, will ring the doorbell and pound on the door as hard as she can. As soon as she hears people moving inside, she'll give us the sign and we'll all run," Eve said.

"That's not a very high-tech plan," her sister complained.

"It's three minutes to midnight. If we want Madison to think Santa dropped off her dog for Christmas, it'll have to do." She didn't like the idea of leaving Bucky outside again, but it would only be for a handful of minutes. If the Hills weren't home or didn't answer, Emily had already said she'd take the dog home with her for the night.

Nick reached through the window and pulled Eve's hand into the cab. He placed his on top of it. "Are we ready to put the final act of Operation Retriever into play?" he asked.

Paul added his hand to the stack. Emily and Helen strained to add theirs. "Go, team!" Emily shouted, causing Bucky to bark. Eve assumed it was in agreement.

"I have some rope in the trunk," Helen offered. She returned a moment later with a length of cord. Bucky's collar was long gone, so Paul held him still as Helen criss-crossed it across the dog's chest to form a halter. It wasn't ideal, but it would last for the short time they needed it.

"You ready, kid?" Eve asked Emily.

"Definitely."

The street was silent. The snow blanketed their footsteps. Bucky strained at the end of his rope, but Nick held it firmly. "I know you want to go home, buddy." He took Eve's hand with his other. "Let's do this."

They left enough slack for Tim and Amanda to bring the dog into the house without untying him. Eve laughed as Nick tied a quadruple knot around the cast iron railings. "I'm not risking him running away again," he whispered. He gave the rope one last pull. "Okay, Emily, you're up."

Emily punched the doorbell three times in a row, until the chimes inside sounded like they were never going to end. She waited half a second before she began pounding on the door, in case she hadn't made enough noise. A light sprang to life in one of the bedroom windows. "Okay, they're awake," she said.

That was when Emily went off-script. She jumped from the steps and shouted, "Ho, ho, ho!" in the deepest voice Eve had ever heard her use. Then she ran.

"Come on!" Nick said. He grabbed her hand and pulled her down the sidewalk, snickering at her stunned face. "I can't believe you didn't see that coming."

Emily paused behind an evergreen at the corner. Nick and Eve crowded behind her.

The Hills' porch light flickered on, and the front door opened, spilling more light onto the steps. Bucky erupted into a flurry of barking. Tim Hill stepped outside in a battered blue robe and slippers. "Maddy! Madison, wake up! Santa's been here."

Tears burned in Eve's eyes. They fell when she heard the little girl's shouts. "It's perfect," she whispered to Nick.

He squeezed her hand in return. "Team Awesome Trucks strikes again."

"And me!" Emily whispered.

"Team Awesome Trucks, assisted by Miss Learner's Licence, strikes again. We made one family's Christmas." Eve felt the full weight of his gaze as Nick spoke the next words straight to her. "Let's get home so we can do it again tomorrow for ourselves."

EPILOGUE

THE SNOW SHONE like a field of diamonds under the early afternoon sun. The unlucky town road crews had worked through the late night and early morning, but the rest of December appreciated the clear streets that ensured everyone made it to their holiday dinners easily.

Nick left Clementine a block away from his cousin's place. Being related didn't guarantee a parking space in the driveway during the open house. His family had a private Christmas breakfast where stockings were emptied and presents unwrapped, and then they opened the doors at noon. That's when he'd taken off to get Eve and lost his parking spot.

It was twelve thirty. Nick and Eve shuffled down the street, their boots adding weight to their feet. He'd been holding her hand since he'd picked her up at her mother's house; now he gave it an extra squeeze. "Are you sure you want to do this? My family can be...intense."

It wasn't that he was against showing Eve off. The problem was the second they walked through the door, his relatives would land on them like the Canadian army on

Juno Beach on D-Day. He didn't want to throw her to the wolves on their first real date.

"Oh, we're doing this. Your cousin promised me shortbread cookies, and I have to beat Adelaide at trivia to show her what a mistake she made not picking me for her team." Eve squeezed back, her massive, black leather mittens muffling the pressure. "You're not going to leave me alone with them, are you?"

"Not a chance."

He led her through the front door, where his cousin's daughter Alicia was playing hostess. She divested them of their coats and shooed them into the living room. Nick took Eve's hand again and headed straight to the instigator. "Gran."

Adelaide clapped her hands in glee, her silver bangles adding a jingle to her joy. "You're wearing matching sweaters. That's adorable."

He'd worn a black sweater with green stripes at the V-neck for the party. Eve had on a green sweater with a black collar and cuffs. She looked so pretty he hadn't said a word about them dressing the same. Now he wished they'd gone back to his place to change. "It wasn't intentional."

His grandmother stared him down. "Uh-huh. Eve, we're thrilled you could come, and that my grandson finally opened his eyes. I think they're playing Twister downstairs. You already missed the speed trivia game."

"I'll get you next year," Eve said.

"I'll look forward to it."

Nick didn't doubt that Eve would be there to beat his grandmother next Christmas. They'd have an entire year to memorize odd, little facts, like whether a yottabyte was bigger or smaller than a zettabyte, or if a platypus was a mammal. He'd researched the last one after Eve had texted him the question that very morning, after she'd said, "*Merry Christmas*."

Half an hour later, when he was rubbing his knee and limping from a pulled hamstring, he added Twister practice to his list of future activities with Eve. She'd taken him down like a pro, which would have been fine if they hadn't been on the same team. He changed his mind and decided to talk to her about sticking to investigating missing pets. They were good at that.

He refilled their punch glasses to wet their parched throats after he'd introduced Eve to yet another set of aunts and uncles. The next couple he ran into needed no introduction.

Amanda Hill threw her arms around Eve's neck. "Thank you, thank you, thank you!" She quickly brushed away a tear from the corner of her eye. "Act surprised."

A second later, Madison came around the corner. "Miss Eve, guess what? Santa brought Bucky home for Christmas. I knew he would!" The little girl wore a bright red headband around her tight black curls. Beside her, Bucky wore a collar in the same shade. "I know you looked hard for him and everything, so thanks, but I told you Santa would take care of it."

Eve laughed. "You told me, alright."

Nick crouched beside the pair. "No more running away from home, Bucky. Everybody was very worried about you," he said to the dog.

Madison shook the leash still attached to his collar. "Mommy says he's going to obedience school as soon as my school starts again. Can we go play now? Mrs. Klassen said they have games."

Nick pointed to the basement door. "Have fun."

Madison was barely around the corner when Amanda threw herself at him. "Thank you, too, Hot Nick."

"It wasn't me. It was Eve and Emily and Paul LeBlanc. I just happened to be around for the grand finale." He patted Amanda's back. "Hot Nick?" he mouthed to Eve, who pinched her lips together and shrugged.

With the arrival of the Hills and the departure of several other guests, they were nudged and jostled toward the entrance to the kitchen. An extra-large, arched opening joined it to the living room. It was wide enough for them to stand face-to-face and still leave enough space for others to get through.

A roar of laugher and a smattering of applause drifted up the stairs. His brothers were throwing elbows at the dessert table over the last butter tart. Across the room, his grandmother, his executive assistant, and his cousin all looked at him and Eve with huge smiles on their faces.

"What do you think of my family's normal, everyday Christmas?" he asked Eve.

"I've always liked the circus," was her quick response.

He laughed at her honesty, because she did like it, and it was a circus. When he glanced across the room again, the interfering trio were staring at him harder. "What?" he shouted.

They all pointed at him.

Nick wrapped his arm around Eve's waist. "Yes, I'm aware I have a date, thank you."

They pointed at him again, then raised their fingers to point up.

He followed the invisible line. "Oh."

Eve looked at him. "Oh, what?"

"Mistle-t-oh." Hanging above them. Not just a cheap, plastic ball, either: a whole bunch of the real stuff.

It had taken them long enough. This wasn't Nick's first time at a Klassen open house. He knew what to look for the second he walked through the door. There was a bunch of mistletoe hanging at the front door, so people coming and going could get a quick peck on the cheek for hellos and good-byes, more over the punch bowl, but Eve hadn't made it to that table yet, and some over the entrance to the kitchen, because everybody went into the kitchen at some point.

It had taken him an hour to get shuffled to this prime spot.

"Oh," Eve said in understanding. "Well."

"My grandmother worked very hard to get us together," Nick said. He leaned a little closer than necessary to speak quietly into her ear. "I'm pretty sure she sabotaged her own car. More than once."

Eve's eyes got big. "Did she now?"

Nick nodded again. "Apparently, I needed many, many shoves in the right direction."

She looked at him again. "Which direction was that?"

"Toward you." Nick leaned forward, and Eve tilted her head a little more. "Merry Christmas, Eve."

"Merry Christmas, Nick."

And then, to the cheers of his family, the Hills, Bucky, who chimed in with a chorus of barking, Eve's mother and sister who'd just arrived, and her father, who had shown up a minute earlier and was still in his coat, Nick finally got to use the mistletoe.

THE END

RECIPE: CONFETTI SQUARES

aka Peanut Butter Marshmallow Squares

Unfortunately, these can't be sent to school because they do contain nuts (I've heard of a Wow-butter version but have not tried it myself.) They are fine – and always popular – at home and work potlucks.

1/2 cup butter
1 cup peanut butter
1 package (300-gram bag) of butterscotch chips
1 bag (200-gram bag) of fruity/multi-coloured mini-marshmallows (you can use white but why be plain?)

Melt the butter, peanut butter and butterscotch chips over a low heat.

Remove and let cool a little as to not melt the marshmallows.

Pour in marshmallows. Stir well to coat thoroughly.

Press into an 8"x8" pan (or a 9"x13" pan for thinner slices). Chill in fridge for 1 hour. You can line the pan with parchment paper for easier removal.

Cut and serve.

RECIPE: CHOCOLATE DROPS

aka Boiled Chocolate Drops or Chocolate Haystacks

1/2 cup butter or margarine (125mL)
1/2 cup milk (125mL)
2 cups granulated sugar (500mL)
1/2 cup cocoa (125mL)
2 1/2 cups rolled/quick oats (625mL) *

Put first four ingredients in a saucepan. Bring to a boil, stirring constantly. Boil for five full minutes.

Remove from heat. Stir in rolled oats. Drop by teaspoon full onto trays covered with waxed paper. Let harden.

Makes 4 dozen.

*Coconut fans can replace 1/2 cup of oats with 2/3 cup of coconut.

RUDY AND KRIS

A North Pole Unlimited Romance
By
Elle Rush

BLURB

Second chances, new romances, and disappearing Secret Santas.

Baker Kris Singleton's hands are full as she covers for her sick aunt at the family bakery. Then she's asked to take her place on a local children's Christmas party committee. Kris has no time for a romance with a former beau who's decided it's time to make up for missed opportunities.

Party chairman Rudy Gillespie knows if he can get Kris's attention again, she'll realize they were always meant to be together. When his plans for the holiday event of the season fall apart, he desperately needs her help to save it from utter disaster.

Can two mismatched elves come together to save Christmas? Only Santa knows.

PROLOGUE

Last week of September
  North Pole Unlimited Headquarters
  December, Manitoba, Canada (25 kilometres south-east of Winnipeg)

Hoots of laughter erupted from the boardroom. Nick Klassen looked at his executive assistant, Jilly Lewis. "We're five minutes late for the meeting, and the inmates have taken over the asylum."

Jilly quirked an eyebrow in response. "Are you surprised?"

"Not really." He knew how the stress of the season affected North Pole Unlimited's staff as they approached their busiest time of the year. Letting them blow off some steam now was good for everyone. As if to prove his point, as soon as they saw him, the mob in the boardroom wrapped up conversations and refilled coffee mugs before they retook their seats. Nick took his chair at the far end of the room, while his cousin, and current company president, North Santana presided from the head of the large, oval table.

"Okay, people, we have a ton to get through today, so let's get to it. It's catalogue finalization day! Again!" North said with half-faked enthusiasm.

Nick was the only person in the room who didn't groan. The company's Christmas catalogue was a huge deal. Planning for it started in February. With less than two months till launch time, they were busy confirming the details. Well, the others were. As VP of Human Resources, he didn't have to worry about filling a section of NPU's digitally-offered selections with products. All he had to do was keep the other departments staffed and on track so they could do the job.

That's when they lost control of the meeting. "Graham, where do we stand with getting Totally Iced back on board? I noticed their contract wasn't renewed after last season. They are coming back, right?" Jilly demanded.

The stout man sitting across from security chief Decker Harkness gulped audibly. Graham Smith combed his fingers through his thinning hair. He ran the Foodservices division, and the Christmas catalogue was heavily weighted with holiday treats. It was Graham's job to ensure North Pole Unlimited had a variety of new edible goodies and old favourites every year. "Actually—" he started to say.

"Actually what? Totally Iced has a chocolate meringue that makes my toes tingle. I order them every Christmas as a present to myself," Jilly said.

Graham gulped again. "As you know, when Sean Fitzwilliam left, that ball got dropped. By the time we got Rudy Gillespie in place, it was too late. We're hoping to have them back for next year's catalogue, but for now, I'm afraid…"

"You should be afraid," Jilly muttered loud enough for Nick to hear.

"I'm sure our man in Calgary can take care of signing them for next year," Graham promised.

"Moving on," North prompted. She addressed the VP of the toy division. "Gabe, how comes the pre-school toy line?"

Nick chuckled. Jilly wouldn't get distracted. She was on a chocolate quest. She'd worked for him for three years, and he had yet to take a single candy from the jar on her desk. He valued his fingers too much.

Graham bolted from the board room the second the meeting was adjourned. Jilly didn't have a chance to corner him. "Leave the man alone. He's doing his best. We'll get you chocolate from somewhere else," Nick said.

"First, no. Nothing compares to Totally Iced," Jilly said. "Second, I'm not saying Graham isn't doing his best, but if he needs help getting them back under the North Pole Unlimited umbrella, I won't let a fellow employee struggle with that alone."

Nick shook his head.

They were in *so* much trouble.

But not as much as the poor people in Alberta.

1. KRIS

The weather outside was frigid, but the heat coming off all the ovens in the Totally Iced Bakery was even worse. Kris Singleton propped open the back door and hoped the convergence of tropical and arctic air wouldn't create a snowstorm in her kitchen.

When the kitchen temperature dropped enough to match to the surface of the sun, Kris got back to work. The morning's cinnamon buns were cooling on the rack. Now she had fruitcakes to make. A bowl of rum-soaked raisins, currants, and cherries sat on the island which dominated the centre of her workspace. A variety of stain-less-steel bowls waited beside the scale on the countertop, and a copy of her grandmother's recipe sat in the clip-beak of a lopsided, yellow ducky card holder.

"I can't believe you're making fruitcake. Does anyone actually eat it?" Marie asked.

"Miss Hauser, are you doubting my skills?" Kris countered, disbelief in her voice.

"I thought fruitcake was something you gave to people you don't like," the blonde assistant baker said. She ducked the swat Kris threw her way.

Kris burst into laughter. "I can't believe you said that." Nobody dissed her grandma's Caribbean fruitcake, especially once they tried it. This was Marie's second year working at the bakery; she ought to know better. "Didn't my aunt send one home with you last year? What happened to it?"

"I gave it to my landlord." Marie brushed her cheek with the back of her wrist, leaving a floury smudge on her face. "He said he liked it," she added in consolation.

"You're definitely eating a slice this year if you want your Christmas bonus," Kris said. "Once you admit you were completely wrong about my amazing family recipe, I expect you to give away samples and convert at least five customers."

"Convert them to the cult of Kris's grandmother's fruitcake?"

"Yes. It's a very tasty cult. I'm its supreme leader and head cheerleader."

"You're a nut, boss."

"Nuts!" Kris had forgotten the walnuts. Fortunately, she had some on hand. The kitchen had everything a baker could ever want. Totally Iced had been her Aunt Vivian's baby since she'd opened the bakery sixteen years earlier, when she'd moved to Calgary.

Kris had only come on board in the last six months. She'd barely gotten her feet under her before the biggest push of the year started. People couldn't get enough of their Christmas dainties. The bakery began gearing up at the beginning of November and the rush lasted to the end of December. All holidays were great for sales, but the Christmas season was extra busy and, for Kris, extra fun. She got to pull out all the seasonal recipes that went into hibernation for ten months of the year. The cookies. The slices.

And the fruitcakes.

The front half of Totally Iced, with its glass display cases and twin bistro tables, didn't open for another hour. It gave her and Marie enough time to weigh ingredients, mix batter, and get the first batch of fruitcakes into the oven. When the last pan slid onto the rack, and she gently closed the heavy, stainless-steel door, Kris broke into a smile. Fruitcake meant Christmas was well and truly on its way.

When the doors opened in time to catch the on-the-way-to-work breakfast crowd, Kris took a break from the kitchen to work the counter.

This morning was the busiest of the week, mostly because it was Two-for-One Cinnamon Bun Tuesday. Half the morning's buns were reserved for local food trucks, but the rest were for their customers. Kris attacked the sugar-addicted horde one person at a time.

"Will you be coming to the party?" she asked a regular who was picking up a birthday cake for her daughter. Kris pointed at the poster in the window, a large white announcement framed in gold and silver garland. The North Calgary Christmas party was *the* children's event for the area, and Totally Iced was one of the sponsors.

"We're already registered," was the quick response.

Kris kept working the line. She didn't notice the black-haired man in the red parka until he stepped to the counter. "Good morning."

"Oh. It's you." She kept her voice flat and fought to keep a smile off her lips.

Rudy Gillespie never missed Two-for-One Cinnamon Bun Tuesday. Or any other day for that matter. He was her best and most loyal customer, but she'd known him long before the first time she saw him stroll through the front door. Years ago, they'd been students at the same college in Toronto. Eight years later, much to both their surprise, he'd walked into Totally Iced in Calgary.

"Kris, you look stunning. As always."

She was well aware of how she looked. After four hours in a hot kitchen, washing her face in the bathroom and doing a quick make-up reapplication before facing customers could only do so much. Kris's fluffy black pony-tail was restrained by a fluorescent pink hair net, which did no favours to her peachy-brown complexion. Her apron was covered in flour and smears from candied fruit, which made it look like she'd spilled a syrup bottle over herself. If beauty was in the eye of the beholder, Rudy needed glasses.

"What can I do for you today, Rudy?"

"A coffee and two cinnamon buns, please."

As she turned to fill his order, Kris caught the smirk he shot to Marie. "Is there something I should know?"

"No, boss."

He lingered after she gave him his change. "You know, coming in every day to ask me out won't change my answer," she told him. No matter how many times or how prettily he asked. She didn't date guys on the rebound.

"I come in because you're the best baker in Alberta." He sounded sincere.

"Flattery like that might work," Marie said.

"Maybe the best baker in the whole country," Rudy amended, to the amusement of the customers still in line.

Marie reached across the counter and high-fived him.

"Traitor," Kris whispered at her.

"On the drive here, I heard *Arrowhead* announced a concert date in Calgary. That's the band you always have playing in the back, right?"

"Not always." She played other bands. Rarely. "But, yes, they're coming to town in the new year."

"Are you going?"

"I wish. I wasn't able to get tickets." The band sold out the Saddledome in a matter of minutes.

"I happen to know a guy who was able to get his hands on a couple tickets. Of course, I'll be using one, but I have a spare. If only I knew somebody else who wanted to go," he said with a sigh. Rudy didn't look her in the eye. He focused all his concentration on his coffee.

Kris had been talking about her dismal lack of ticket luck the day before with Marie. They'd been the only two people in the building. She whirled, shaking her finger in the assistant baker's face. "*J'accuse!* You're collaborating with him against me."

"What can I say, boss? One of you can help me get the year's number one toy for my niece, and the other is you." Marie slapped Rudy's upraised hand again.

"Nice try, Rudy, but no," Kris said. Although it was the most tempting offer he'd made to date. Not that she needed bribes to go out with him. The desire to say yes was already there. It was the other reasons.

"Okay. I'll keep asking around. Let me know if you change your mind. If it's not too late," he added. He grabbed the white paper bag containing his cinnamon buns and toasted her and Marie with his coffee. "My spare, sixth-row ticket and I will see you tomorrow," he said on his way out the door.

The rest of the people flowed through the store quickly after their main source of entertainment left. When it emptied, Kris advanced on Marie. "You've been feeding Rudy ideas on how to get me to say yes?"

"He's a good guy."

"He is," Kris agreed.

"And, technically, no, I haven't been giving ideas to Rudy, although they seem to get to him eventually. What's your problem with him anyway?"

"His taste in women."

The bell over the door jingled and Vivian Singleton strode in like she owned the joint. Which she did. Her aunt's heart attack in the summer had taken her out of the shop and put her on bed rest. Kris had agreed to manage Totally Iced's day-to-day operations until she was back on her feet. The doctor told Vivian she needed to cut back on stress and exertion; since Kris was between jobs, it was perfect timing. If Kris got the bakery through the Christmas season, her aunt planned to take back the reins in the new year.

Vivian had more grey in her hair than she'd had a year ago—streaks running from her temple to the sparse bun at the back of her head. "How are we doing, girls?"

"Great, Aunt Viv. Today's cinnamon buns are ready for the food truck pick-ups, and the fruitcakes are in the oven. Next up is—"

"Gingerbread," her aunt said. "I'm glad you're keeping to my schedule. I was hoping you'd need a hand with the decorating."

"The doctor said—"

"The doctor said no stress. Putting frosting and sprinkles on cookies is the opposite of stressful. I'll be back after lunch," Vivian interrupted again.

Kris knew her aunt was going stir-crazy. It had been bad enough over the summer when she puttered around the yard, but now that was under six inches of snow. "Okay, we'll see you then."

Now that she was done with Kris, Vivian turned to Marie. "How is my niece's suitor doing?"

"He offered to take her to a concert, but she turned him down," Marie snitched.

"Why did you say no?" her aunt demanded.

Kris wondered exactly how many people Marie had been talking to. "Because I don't want to start something I won't be around to see through," she explained, and it was part of the truth. "Rudy's a great guy. He deserves somebody who can appreciate that long term, and I don't have the time to be that person." She didn't know how long it would take him to get over his ex, but it was longer than she had left in Calgary. It was a shame; she liked him.

"We'll have to work on your attitude. And your love life," her aunt said.

"Yes, we will," Marie agreed.

"No, it's okay," Kris protested.

"Don't worry, Kris, we're happy to help."

That's what worried her.

2. RUDY

THE CINNAMON BUN was worth adding twenty minutes to his morning commute. To be honest, seeing Kris was worth the twenty minutes on her own. The delicious morning treat was only extra incentive.

He handed the bag and remaining bun to his second-in-command. "You owe me."

"I don't think so. I'm the one who gave you the tip about the Arrowhead tickets." Tucker Abraham ripped the white bag down the side and transferred the cinnamon bun to a plate. Then he began cutting it into bite-sized pieces with a knife and fork.

"What are you doing? Eating with the Queen?" Rudy asked.

"I'm savouring, not stuffing it in my mouth one-handed while I'm driving." To emphasize his point, Tucker speared a particularly gooey piece loaded with raisins and put it in his mouth. "Mmm mmm good," he said as he chewed it, staring directly at Rudy.

Maybe his assistant had the right idea—making the

sweet bun last like that. Now Rudy regretted rushing through his. "See if I ever bring you another one."

When Rudy had first arrived at the North Pole Unlimited western Canadian hub, Tucker had been on the verge of a medical leave. His original boss, Sean Fitzwilliam, had gone to Las Vegas and never returned after winning a slot machine jackpot. Tucker had been trying to do his job and cover the manager's duties at the same time. Rudy transferred in three weeks later, and his first act had been to order Tucker to take a much-needed four-day weekend.

That's when they'd discovered Fitz had been letting things slide long before he'd left for vacation, one of the results of which was letting the long-time Totally Iced contract lapse. Rudy found an ancient to-do list buried in the files. It was what had originally sent him to the bakery. Then he learned about Vivian Singleton's heart attack and Kris stepping in. Rudy let it go, figuring everyone had moved on, which was a shame, because losing Totally Iced left a hole in the hearts and stomachs of long-time customers.

Which led Rudy back to the cinnamon buns. He should have bought four.

"Are you telling me you don't want to know which author's book Kris is waiting for? Because I've got a call scheduled with Marie later," Tucker continued.

"I'll bring you another one tomorrow."

"Thanks. By the way, you have two messages you want, and one you don't. You also asked me to remind you about the Christmas party board meeting this afternoon. Shout if you need me while I'm enjoying this fine cinnamon bun."

Rudy put the delectable baker out of his mind for the

time being. The concert tickets had been the latest in a long line of unsuccessful attempts to get Kris to say yes to a date. He needed a new approach. With North Pole Unlimited approaching its busiest season, he was afraid he'd have to put his plans on hold until the new year, and he had already waited for her long enough.

He flipped through the message sheets and stopped when he got to the one from head office. He'd reported back to December regularly when he inherited the mess in Calgary with his transfer and promotion, but those calls had become fewer and further between. He couldn't imagine what they were checking on now, unless there was a problem with the extra seasonal help he'd hired.

He emailed Nick Klassen to let him know he was back in the office, but instead of a phone call, his computer screen beeped with an incoming video call.

Rather than the close-up of one person's face, Rudy found himself looking at the wide shot of three people huddled around a desk: Nick Klassen, the VP of Human Resources who had to approve his staffing paperwork; Jilly Lewis, Nick's assistant; and, oddly, Graham Smith. Rudy recognized him from the company's website, but he had no idea why the vice-president of Foodservices would be in on a call with him.

"Rudy, are you familiar with the Totally Iced Bakery in Calgary?" Graham asked.

"Yes."

"And their relationship with North Pole Unlimited?"

"I am, to the extent that there currently isn't a relationship, since Fitz didn't sign them to participate in this year's catalogue."

Jilly slapped Graham in the arm. "I told you so," she said.

"Sean was supposed to contact them months ago," Graham said. Jilly poked him, and he stopped speaking long enough to glare at her until she retreated to her chair. "Although it's too late for the catalogue, we still want them to participate in the Twelve Sales for Christmas promotion. I'm sure they'll be amenable."

"I doubt it," Rudy said.

"Why?"

"Because Vivian Singleton had a heart attack a few months ago. Her niece Kris has temporarily taken over the bakery."

"I heard about that, but I also heard that she was doing well. Is Vivian not back yet?" Jilly asked.

"Not till the new year, so they're still shorthanded. We can't ask them to take on a contract that generally has a three-month production time and ask them to do it in four weeks. Do you know how many cookies that is?"

"Four hundred dozen, or four thousand eight hundred delectable chocolate meringues," Jilly said without hesitation. When they all stared at her in stunned silence, she stared back. "What part of 'these cookies are very important to me' was unclear?"

"As important as they may be, you do understand that I'd be approaching them cold for a holiday season treat *in the middle of the holiday season*. I don't think it's realistic to expect a yes," Rudy said.

"Then make it realistic. I want my meringues!"

"Jilly, cool it," Nick ordered. "Sorry, Rudy. Will you make the offer anyway? We could fly Hollis Dash in to deliver the contract, but since you're in the area and already know them, you could save us a few steps, and possibly a few days."

Rudy wasn't going to turn down a chance to see Kris,

even if he already knew what her answer would be. "Sure, send it."

Graham looked relieved, but exhausted. "Thank you, Rudy. We'll email it to you this afternoon." When Jilly coughed, loudly, Graham corrected himself. "I mean we'll send it this morning."

Jilly leaned right into the camera. "You're wonderful, Rudy," she said. "If you need my help with anything, anything at all, ask me. I'll be right there. Please send my good wishes to Vivian for a continued speedy recovery."

After that conversation, the rest of the morning went smoothly, until Tucker interrupted. "Rudy? Cynthia is on line one again. She said to tell you specifically it's about today's committee meeting," Tucker called from his desk in the other room.

"Put her on hold for a minute."

He needed longer than that. Cynthia Quinn tried his patience in an entirely different way than Kris. The pretty baker was a challenge in a fun, exciting way. Cynthia was a challenge in a 'try to remember, homicide carries a life sentence' kind of way, and he couldn't seem to get away from her.

He didn't understand why the woman had joined the North Calgary Christmas Party committee in the first place. Cynthia didn't like kids, thought volunteering was a waste of her time, and had told him more than once she thought Christmas was best spent on a beach. When he'd asked why she was making herself miserable, Cynthia admitted she wanted to get her new party-coordinator business some exposure in the community.

He, on the other hand, had been excited to step into the role in Fitz's absence. Not only did Rudy like the idea of paying back the community centre he'd played in as a kid, he'd also held similar volunteer positions in the past, so he knew what he was getting into.

At least it wasn't a conference call with the third member of the committee. Warren Massey was in charge of the Present Project and wasn't any better. He had only managed to attend two of the last ten meetings on time. The man seemed to think handing out a box of swag covered in company logos was the beginning and end of his responsibilities. Thankfully the fourth member, Jennifer Chang, was an experienced committee leader who had the parent volunteers well in hand.

He took a breath and pressed the button. "Hello, Cynthia."

"You have to help me, Rudy. *That woman* is insisting we serve hot dogs and chips to the children. I don't want to do hot dogs. I suggested a nice mushroom risotto. When she said no to that, I compromised to charcuterie, so she could have her "finger food", but that wasn't good enough either."

That woman was Kris, who had taken her aunt's place as the fifth and final person on the committee. Even if he weren't in hot pursuit, he would have sided with her on this argument. "Cynthia, kids don't want risotto or char-cuterie. They want hot dogs and chips and juice boxes and cookies."

"But hot dogs! Couldn't we at least do a nice bratwurst and some artisanal or Dijon mustard?"

Yes, because all preschoolers would prefer Dijon over ketchup. "You can mention it, but the menu choices were approved by Jennifer, and the parents' representative, two meetings ago. It's too late to change things now." Not that she'd stop trying.

Rudy liked the idea of the community party. He got a

kick out of it on a personal level. A bunch of sugared-up kids running around cheering for Santa put him in the Christmas spirit quicker than anything else. The North Calgary Community Christmas party had always existed; always being as far back as he could remember. He was honoured to be a part of it. The fact it was good for business was a distant second. North Pole Unlimited was all about making Christmas special; supporting the event had been an easy decision for the company.

"You'll be at the meeting?"

"Yes, I'll be there." He had to be; he was the committee chair. It was his job to ensure all the food, presents and party events were on track. With less than a month to go, it was all about the details at this point.

"Maybe we could go out for drinks after to discuss the menu," Cynthia suggested.

"I already have plans," he said. He'd make some if he had to.

"We'll see. Looking forward to seeing you, Rudy." She ended the call before he could correct her.

"Aargh!"

"Boss?"

"I will pay you to run over my foot to get me out out of that meeting. Nothing too debilitating, just a couple toes." He could limp for a week. He wouldn't mind.

"Sorry, Rudy, I can't help you. Besides, you need to be there."

"Why?" Aside from the kids depending on him for a holiday party, the corporate sponsorships he'd already taken money for, and the fact he'd given his word to participate, he couldn't think of a single reason why he had to go.

"A little birdy told me Kris will need probably some

extra support," Tucker said. His assistant looked at him, eyes big and guileless. "But you have your own problems to worry about."

"Clear my schedule. Nothing is keeping me from that meeting."

3. KRIS

KRIS'S BOOTS gripped the packed snow as she crossed the parking lot, announcing her presence with a squeak each time she took a step. Calgary weather was unpredictable at the best of times, but this November had been persistently and unrelentingly cold. A blizzard at the beginning of the month had dropped six inches of snow, and they still had all of it. Kris still held out hope for a Chinook to melt it before Christmas, but it wasn't looking good. Winter was here to stay until at least March.

It would give them a white Christmas, though, and that was something to look forward to. It had snowed when she lived in Toronto, but that was a heavy, damp snow that permeated to the bone. Calgary was a dry cold, and yes, to her surprise, it did make a difference.

The bakery was closed for the day, and she should be on her way home, but this job was an unexpected addition to her regular duties; she had to replace Aunt Vivian and her commitments to the local community centre. In the summer, it had only been a few hours a week. As the holidays grew closer, Kris constantly added meetings and tasks to her to-do list. She didn't mind. It was for a good cause, and it gave her more opportunities to see Rudy.

The committee met in one of the centre's bare-bones meeting rooms, which consisted of a table and half a dozen chairs. Rudy called the group to order, reviewed the minutes from the last meeting, and opened the floor to new business.

Warren spoke first. "I bought a bunch of toques which were on sale for the gift bags, and I found a bulk place to purchase candy canes. That should be good enough."

"No. We have a budget, and Jennifer sent everyone copies of what needs to be purchased. This was the job you signed on for, Warren. You can't back out now," Rudy said.

"Fine. I'll try to get to it this week."

"Excellent. I'll let our sponsoring stores know to expect your call." At first, Kris had deferred to the other committee member, trusting him to get it done. The last month had taught her to be proactive.

"What about hiring a Santa for the party?" Rudy asked.

"I called everyone on the list you gave me." An exasperated look crossed Warren's face. "I even used my work contacts, but I couldn't find a single available St. Nick. I'm expanding my search to Airdrie and Okotoks. I'll go all the way to Red Deer if I have to. You'd think those character actor people would appreciate the opportunity for such a good corporate gig for a couple hours work."

"You'd think," Rudy said, and Warren nodded.

Kris had no idea how Warren missed the sarcasm.

"Next. Food. Kris, we finalized the menus at the last meeting. How goes finding a supplier?"

She quickly pulled out her own notes. "We're good. I confirmed the meal with Jennifer and the parents' group last week. I'm ordering everything through Totally Iced's suppliers, and I'll hand in the receipts after the party for reimbursement."

"Hot dogs and hamburgers and buns and condiments," Cynthia commented with a sneer. "I'm still not sure about that. A friend of mine has a catering company and would be happy to do all the cooking and serving. They include the tablecloths, napkins and chafing dishes in their quote. I can have numbers for you next week."

"We have a crew of volunteer parents for that, Cynthia," Rudy reminded her.

"But this will be much easier. They'll give us a discount. You'll see when you get the quote. We should hold off on any orders until then."

Kris was surprised Rudy wasn't drawing blood at how hard he was biting his tongue. "Anything else?" he asked.

"Yes. I'm concerned over the lack of vegan dishes," Cynthia continued.

Kris grimaced. She really didn't want to do what she was about to do, but it was important. "That's a good point, Cynthia."

"It is? Thank you." For the first time that meeting, Cynthia looked her in the eye. "My friend suggested some sweet potato canapés topped with a tomato and shallot chutney, and some stuffed mushroom caps. Oh, and he has the most delightful avocado gazpacho! They will really take the party to the next level."

"Actually, I was thinking more of having some vegetarian burgers and soy dogs available on request. Maybe a carrot stick and celery tray with some dip." Cynthia looked ready to kill her. Kris felt better. "But it was an insightful comment, and I'll mention it to the parents' committee. Thank you for considering that part of the community. I should have thought of it myself."

She should have. In fact, she pulled out her phone and made a note for herself to see what the bakery was planning for that segment of the customers.

"Cynthia, you're in charge of the games and entertainment. How are you doing with that? Do you need a hand?" Rudy asked.

"I'm perfectly capable of entertaining school children."

Kris had her doubts. Apparently, so did Rudy. "Let us know if you change your mind and would like some help."

"I won't."

Rudy brought the meeting to a close. Warren left grumbling threats to non-existent uncooperative Santas everywhere, while Cynthia muttered about Kris. It didn't have a very Christmas-like feel. "Kris, can you wait a minute? I'll walk you to your car." She was about to turn him down when he continued. "I want to ask your opinion about something."

Kris lingered outside the community centre, her nose getting colder by the second. She shook her head when he finally appeared with Cynthia by his side.

She put her hand on his arm, and he shook his head. She removed it, and he shook his head again, pointing at Kris. Then the brunette glared at *her* and stomped toward her car.

"Am I keeping you from something important?" Kris asked.

"No. That was..." His voice trailed off and he waved his hands. "Cynthia being Cynthia. I wanted to ask you how you felt about the party."

"I'm concerned, to be honest. We're running out of time, and there's tons left to do."

"I think we'll be fine. We still have a few weeks to iron out the rough spots."

"We don't have a Santa. Cynthia is going to keep pushing her friend the caterer. Despite what she said, I'm certain she hasn't even started looking at entertainment."

He glanced over his shoulder. "You're probably right. We might be in trouble. Do you want to go out for a drink and discuss contingencies?"

"Absolutely."

4. RUDY

KRIS WAS all talk and no alcohol as Rudy watched her inhale a tray of thick cut French fries, a veggie burger, and a root beer. He laughed when she said the veggie patty was research. He had a cheeseburger, side salad, and milk shake; he had to go back to work and needed to fuel what was sure to be a long night.

"What have you been doing since Toronto?" Kris asked over their impromptu meal.

"That seems like a lifetime ago." Rudy had been born and raised in Calgary. He'd moved to Ontario to try living out east. His first year of college had been an adventure. He toughed out the second because he was too stubborn to quit. For the most part, he hadn't enjoyed it. Everything was too crowded and too expensive, and he'd missed the mountains. The minute he'd completed his Logistics program, he'd hightailed it home and happily returned to his roots.

It hadn't been all bad. He'd made a lot of friends at college, most of them through various sports teams. He first met Kris through the college's co-ed soccer league, but he hadn't truly gotten to know her until they were on the same dodgeball team. Kris had been a quick, agile, and most importantly, vicious player. He admired that in a teammate.

"Earth to Rudy?"

"Sorry. I moved back after graduation. My family is here, and most of my friends. Calgary is booming, so I've never had to look elsewhere for work. How about you?"

Kris shrugged. "Bakeries are finicky places. All four places I worked at in Toronto closed down within two years of me starting with them. I only came to Calgary to help after my aunt's heart attack. Once she's back on her feet, I'll have to move back east. Most of my family is there. I miss my sister like crazy." She patted her phone when she said it.

Rudy knew what it was like to be so far from family. It wasn't fun. He was glad both his younger brother and sister lived in town. "You've been in Calgary for five months. Have you made any new connections? Tracked down old friends?"

"Not yet. I haven't gotten around to it."

That didn't sound like Kris. She'd always been outgoing. He knew she'd been working hard, but everybody needed something beyond their jobs. "Are you on a dodgeball team yet?"

She raised one eyebrow. "You have a league here?"

"A big one. If you want some introductions, I can probably find a team that needs a substitute player until you can register for a full session in January." Whoever got her should consider themselves lucky; Kris had wicked aim.

"Please do. That sounds like fun." Her smile blinding. "I've missed throwing things at people, and that is something you can only say to another dodgeball person."

He laughed, because it was true. "Have you made any other ties in Calgary?"

"Church, of course. My aunt's congregation was very welcoming, although it's very small. I've spent most of my time at Totally Iced. We've been non-stop, and it's getting even busier. Aunt Vivian's bakery has become one of the go-to spots for local businesses when it comes to client gifts. Her chocolate meringues and sugar cookies sell out all the time." She paused to sip her root beer. "But I'm pleased to say my own personal recipe for chocolate drizzled cranberry orange shortbread is also doing very well. Everything is going great, but we may need more help soon."

"That's a good problem to have." He wouldn't get a better opening than that. "Speaking of good problems..."

"Do we have to discuss problems tonight? We were having such a nice meal."

"Good problems," he repeated. "I got a call from North Pole Unlimited Head Office in December. They were hoping you would like to renew your contract with them."

"Sure. Aunt Vivian was disappointed when they didn't ask her this year."

He was shocked. He hadn't expected it to be so easy. "Fantastic." That's when it all fell apart.

"If we start planning now, we can come up with something exciting for next year. We'll have months to test recipes."

"Um, no. They want you back for a special promotion *this* year."

"This year? As in *this* Christmas? The one happening

in less than two months?" She set down her glass. "Are you crazy? Do you know how many cookies that would entail?"

"Four thousand eight hundred, according to a person who would know."

"Do you know how long that will take to make?"

"Hopefully about three weeks," he quipped. Then Rudy got serious. "Is it possible? Could you get more help like you were talking about and do it?"

"I don't think so. Even with an extra person, we couldn't handle that volume."

"What about two extra people?" he teased. Kind of. Jilly scared him.

"I'll speak to Aunt Vivian," Kris promised.

"And I won't mention it again tonight." Because he needed to work on his arguments on why Totally Iced should break their backs for his company. It didn't sound like they needed the business. "If I happen to come across someone looking for a holiday baking gig, can I send them your way?"

"That would be acceptable."

He'd look for two bakers. But before he started looking, he had something more important to do. "Would you like to go out for dinner sometime?"

Kris waved at their plate as she popped another fry in her mouth.

"No, this was a commiseration meal after dealing with a miserable committee meeting. I'm talking about a real date."

She gulped, hard, then took a deep pull on her root beer. "What about Cynthia?"

"She's not invited. She and I had one date, and it went about as well as you'd expect. I keep turning her down, hoping she'll stop asking. After today, maybe she will."

Well, Kris thought. If Cynthia wasn't in the picture, that changed things. Some of the things, anyway. "Okay. Let's try it."

5. KRIS

"BOSS, DELIVERY FOR YOU!"

Kris was wrist-deep in her last batch of shortbread for the day when Marie shouted from the front of the shop. She washed her hands twice to get rid of all the flour and butter before she walked out to sign for the day's packages. "Please tell me it's the supplies we ordered," she said.

"Umm. Maybe?" Marie held the door open for the delivery guy with the hand truck. The snowflake-dotted man wheeled in a towering load of brown cardboard boxes. That was in addition to the piles already stacked in front of their display case.

Kris recognized the logo on the side of the boxes. It was from the packaging company they used to send Totally Iced's goodies through the mail. But then the delivery guy went back for another load. "Wait a minute. We only ordered two boxes of trays and containers," she protested.

"Twenty-two," he corrected.

"No, two. We'll never go through twenty. That's a year's worth of supplies. There must be some mistake."

"I have more in the van for you if you want to double-check your invoice, but I'm telling you, the delivery chit says twenty-two."

Kris sprinted to the office and called up the online order she'd submitted the previous week. She was right. She'd only requested two boxes. But in the purchase history on the company's site, there was another order. For twenty more. And it wasn't hers.

She quickly reached for the phone. "Good afternoon, Aunt Viv. Did you order twenty boxes of packing supplies without telling me?"

The pause at the other end of the line could have meant many things, but the gasp was the answer. "Oh, nuts! That's my standing annual North Pole Unlimited order. I completely forgot to cancel it."

That could be a sign, especially if she was considering taking on the order. "Don't worry. We can always send them back. I'll deal with it. Are you coming in tomorrow?"

"I can."

"I'd appreciate it. I have some news for you."

"Then I'll be there."

One problem solved. The other was stacking up on the other side of the front counter. By the time she left her office, the guy was bringing in a third load, with two different, long, flat ones balanced on top. These boxes had red and green bows printed in the lower right-hand corners, and Kris didn't recognize the logo. "What are these?"

"I don't know. I just deliver them."

"I didn't order anything from that company," Kris protested.

"To Kris Kringleton, care of Totally Iced Bakery, Calgary. That's you, right?"

"Mostly." It was her name on the shipping order, overlooking the error, and the address was correct. But she had no idea what was inside.

"It looks like Christmas came early," Marie said when Kris opened the first box.

"Be nice or I'll make you wear it," Kris threatened. It was a vicious lie, but they both laughed.

Neither of them would be caught dead in the elf costumes. There were four: two male and two female. Kris was glad to see they were equally non-discriminate horrific green tunics and knee-length shorts. The women had red and white striped stockings, whereas the men had bright yellow ones. Both sets had green felt boot covers with curly toes.

"It's like Santa's workshop fell into a Tim Burton wardrobe warehouse nightmare," Marie said, her voice quiet with shock.

"Elf prison wear," Kris agreed. She slapped the flaps of the box closed. "We have to get these out of the store. If Aunt Vivian sees these, she'll make us wear them until Christmas."

As if she knew Kris wasn't joking, Marie ducked behind the counter and returned with a roll of tape. "Quick."

A lull hit the radio, flooding the bakery with a silence deep enough they heard a car pull up beside the store. The squeak of the snow under the tires was only a whisper, but they caught it. "It's her. She said tomorrow," Kris whispered. "Get rid of this!"

Marie tossed the costume box into the storage room, then threw a container box on it. The two of them piled half a dozen more boxes on top of that and heard the bell above the door jingle while they continued to bury the evidence.

"Hello?" a male voice called from the front.

"Oh, thank goodness. It's only Rudy," Kris said.

"I'll take a minute to organize this," Marie promised. "Your aunt won't dig to the bottom of the pile. The doctor told her no heavy lifting."

"That sounds like a plan. I'll call the company tomorrow and get a label to send those fashion disasters back." Kris snickered. The outfits were funny. They'd be hilarious if they'd been sent to her aunt while Kris was visiting, but then she wouldn't have been able to laugh. Her aunt had taught her how to throw a dodgeball.

She peeked at the bathroom mirror when she walked by. Her face was flushed from panic, but her eyes were bright. When she greeted Rudy, he stared at her grin. "What's so funny?" he asked.

"I received twenty-two boxes of shipping supplies instead of the two I wanted, because my aunt didn't cancel the standing order for the North Pole Unlimited shipment we don't have to make. Plus, there was another odd delivery. Marie is trying to wrangle all the boxes into the storage room. I hope she's good at Tetris."

"I am," the junior baker yelled. "Okay, these are put away for now. Do you want me to finish the shortbread?"

"No. I'll cover it and finish it tomorrow."

"Do you need a few more minutes? We have some time before our reservation," Rudy said.

"Nope, I'm ready now." She'd been ready for days. "I do need a minute to change." She couldn't go out with

Rudy the night after he asked; this was the soonest they'd been able to manage. It would be her first real date in Calgary. When Kris first arrived, she'd been too busy to socialize. There was a brief period where she considered dipping her toe in the dating pool, but since she wasn't planning to stay, she didn't search very hard. And then Rudy had appeared.

She had a new sweater she'd been saving for a special occasion. She paired the gold knit top with a chunky amber necklace, which set off her dark skin. She added a pair of thick, lined wool slacks. Her black leather dress boots finished the outfit. She'd fit into whatever restaurant Rudy surprised her with.

He was muttering when she returned with her coat. He slapped the remote on his keychain into his palm, then squeezed one of the buttons. "What's wrong?" she asked.

"My car won't start."

"We can take mine." She paused. "No, we can't." Her car was in the shop overnight. She'd planned to take the bus home to get ready for their date until Rudy said he'd meet her at the bakery.

Rudy's shoulders slumped. "I'll call for an Uber to get us to the restaurant. Then I'll call for a tow truck after."

That was a terrible plan. He'd be waiting till the wee small hours for the tow truck, plus he'd be outside in the freezing cold. "You should call them first. We'll eat later." Even if they lost their reservations, there were dozens of restaurants they could walk right into. "I don't mind."

"I do. This is our first date. I was supposed to wow you with scintillating conversation over romantic candlelight."

"I promise to still be wowed." How could she not be

when he was obviously going to so much effort to impress her? "Give them a call."

He tapped on the screen for a moment, then growled at his phone again. "They must be swamped. They're giving me a two- to six-hour window for the tow-truck. Let's leave it. The car will still be here when we get back."

Flakes floated past the large front windows. Kris had forgotten a storm was moving in. "Your car could be buried by morning." She set her purse on the table. Then she gave the round, glass-topped table another look. "You know, we could have a quiet dinner for two right here while we wait."

She saw Rudy study the floorspace at the front of the shop. The display cases were dark and mostly empty. She'd already turned out all the lights, so the only illumination came from the glow of the green neon band around the clock, the red "Exit" signs, and the street lights shining through the window. "I think we have candles in the back, too, if you're still planning on the romantic part of the evening," she offered.

"That's sweet, but I don't want you to have to settle for something like that."

"Who's settling? The most important part is that we'll be having dinner together."

Kris blushed. Thankfully the room was too dim for Rudy to see it. She hadn't meant to speak that thought aloud. There was such a thing as being too eager.

Although Rudy didn't seem to think so. "We could order in." He dipped his face toward his phone screen again. "I'll have everything ordered and on its way in five minutes."

"What are my options?" She didn't like it when a man

ordered for her. She was perfectly capable of making her own decisions.

"I'm not telling." He glanced at her. "Don't worry, you'll still get to choose what you want. I'll order one of everything and let you pick from that."

She unwrapped her scarf and unbuttoned her coat. Her movements must have caught Rudy's eye, because he looked at her again. Then he smiled for the first time since their date plans had gone south. "You look stunning."

Kris smiled back before she could stop herself. "Thank you." It was nice to get dressed up, but nicer to have her efforts appreciated.

When Rudy took off his own coat, she saw he'd also dressed to impress. All she'd seen him in was jeans and work shirts, which made sense, because warehouses were dusty places. For tonight, he'd worn a nice dress shirt and sports coat. She couldn't make out the design on his tie until she stepped closer. It was tiny white snowflakes on a navy background. "You look very handsome, yourself."

By the time they hunted down the candles and moved the table away from the draft coming through the window, their meal arrived, and Kris still didn't know where they were supposed to eat. Rudy spread the containers across the table. He grimaced at the paper plates and disposable cutlery, but Kris didn't flinch at it when he pushed her chair in for her.

She finally caught a glimpse of the restaurant logo. "I've seen that place. It's on Kensington. I haven't tried it."

He popped the lid on the first container. "My sister Rebecca loves tapas. She drags me here every few months. I've yet to be disappointed. You did say you liked small plates, right?"

"Absolutely." Kris fell in love with the wide world of

cheese when she hit college, especially once her pastry and baking classes traded finished products with the chef courses. When she saw the trays Rudy set around the table, she swallowed hard. "It looks amazing."

She didn't realize how fast time flew until the room filled with a yellow flashing light. "The tow truck is here."

The wall clock said two hours had passed. It felt like a minute. A few crumbs lingered in the bottom of the take-out containers. The rest of their meal—like their conversation—was a pleasant memory.

"I should go out and see what's wrong," Rudy continued.

"I'll clean this up," she offered.

"Absolutely not." Rudy scooped the containers and plates and dropped them into the brown paper bag the meal came in. "All done. I'll sort out the recycling later. Come on, I'll drive you home if they can get my car started."

For the second time that night, Kris reached for her coat. But this time, Rudy held her it as she slipped her arms into the sleeves, and he held her purse as she buttoned it.

The snow was falling heavier than ever when they got outside. Kris carefully locked the bakery door behind her. The streetlight's beam lit the side of Rudy's face, highlighting half of his smile. "Thanks for going with the changes this evening. I'll plan something extra special for the next time I take you out."

"Oh, no. Next time I'm taking you out."

"I'll hold you to that." He leaned closer. Then they both jumped when the tow truck driver reminded them he was there. "Hey, buddy, which car is yours?"

That broke the mood, and they were too cold to get it

back by the time the guy got Rudy's car started. But when Rudy drove away after dropping her off, she was smiling. She was thrilled he'd agreed to a second date. Although now she had to top a snowed-in, romantic dinner.

She had work to do.

6. RUDY

"LOOK OUT!"

"It's getting away!

"Quick, grab it before it hits the door!"

Rudy's arms were covered in strips of cello tape, and his index fingers were on two different packages, holding ribbons in place until the final knots were tied. When he accidentally knocked the spool off the table with his elbow, he expected it to land at his feet, not to try to escape from the gift-wrapping committee.

Kris plucked a piece of tape from his sleeve. "Try to keep the supplies on the table, Gillespie. We still have over a hundred books to wrap. We'll need every inch of that stuff."

"Okay, tissue paper whisperer."

She stuck the tape on his mouth, then broke into giggles.

They had an assembly line going in the community centre and were halfway through the two hundred gift bags they needed. Jennifer labelled the bags and managed the list. Two other parents ensured each kid got a candy cane and a donated toque Warren had supplied. A third parent and Kris wrapped the small, individual presents and the books and handed them back to Jennifer as soon as they were done.

After three paper cuts and one pair of dropped scissors in the first five minutes, Rudy was reassigned to be the tape holder and designated gopher.

He had never seen so much wrapping paper in his life. Rolls of it. Stacks of rolls. Kris wielded scissors like a knight did a sword. Blades flashed, paper flew, and he attached more strips of tape to his arm.

When his phone rang, he ducked into the hall. The baby-blue-painted cinder blocks covered with ice schedules for the various hockey and ringette teams temporarily distracted him from the screen. "Hello?"

"Rudy, it's Warren."

"Warren! Where are you?"

"I'm bowing out of the community Christmas party committee."

Rudy blinked at his phone. "What?"

"I wish you all the best. I'm sure it'll be a success. You can keep the toques."

The hats were the least of Rudy's concerns. "You're not really quitting, are you? We need you. The party is in a month. What about Santa?"

"Yeah, sorry. I wasn't able to find one."

"Then you ask for help and pitch in somewhere else. You can't just walk out."

"Actually, I can. Good luck."

Then there was nothing. Who did that? Who disappointed a neighbourhood full of children right before a Christmas party? Even worse, not only had Warren left them shorthanded for present wrapping, he hadn't managed to do the most important task he'd been assigned. "This is a disaster."

"What is?"

He hadn't heard Kris sneak up behind him. "Warren quit."

"Quit what?"

"The committee."

"He can't do that." Her hands fluttered as she raised them to her throat. "We need him. He can quit later. After the party."

"That's not all."

"It gets worse?" she asked.

"He didn't arrange for Santa's visit." That had always been the best part of the party when he was a kid. Little Rudy had walked around for a week with his chest puffed out after Santa called his name and said he had heard that Rudy had been a good boy. St. Nick telling him to continue the good work was the primary reason his parents had such a well-behaved boy for the month of December.

Forget about the kids, the parents would be devastated at the news.

He should be thankful for the utterly disappointed look on Kris's face. It would be good practice for facing all the kids. "Santa's not coming? What are we going to do?" Kris whispered. He hated the tears in her voice.

He was going to fix it. If anybody had connections for the Big Man in Red, it would be somebody at North Pole Unlimited. "I'll take care of it. I'll call my head office. I'm sure they know somebody who knows somebody who can get a hold of the guest of honour."

"But it's so late in the season! Finding a hole in a schedule will be impossible. I mean, getting elves to help hand out the gifts isn't a problem. But Santa." She shook her head in defeat.

Kris was right. But he faked confidence he didn't have. "It's the holidays. It's the time for Christmas miracles. Don't worry. I've got this. This party isn't happening without Santa."

A quiet, high-pitched gasp froze them to their spots. Kris's eyes went wide, and Rudy was sure his matched as he replayed the conversation in his head, trying to think if he'd forever ruined Christmas for some youngster because he hadn't thought about being overheard. They turned around slowly.

"You know somebody who knows Santa? And he's coming to our party?" A little boy, too young for school, with straight black hair and dark brown eyes gazed at them.

"You bet, little man. He'll be here to deliver the presents," Rudy promised. He crossed his heart with his finger.

Behind the child, Jennifer watched with a huge grin on her face. "Nice save," she mouthed.

"Thanks," he replied silently.

Jennifer crouched beside the little boy. "I'm pretty sure you're supposed to be in Kinder-gym, Lee."

"But, Mom, Santa!"

"The grown-ups are dealing with Santa. Your job is to do your best at gymnastics and have fun at the party." She held up four fingers and the little boy copied her.

"Four more Saturdays and then we can have a party?"

"Then we can have a fantastic party." Jennifer took his hand. "I'll be back once I return him to class," she said over her shoulder as she herded her son down the hall.

"Take your time. We'll get back to work," Kris said.

She pulled Rudy out of the hall and closed the door firmly behind him. Then locked it. "That was terrifying."

He tugged his sweaty t-shirt away from his chest. "I thought we blew it for a second."

"You'd better come through now, Rudy. Your reputation is on the line."

Didn't he know it.

7. KRIS

TOTALLY ICED HIT a lull at half past three. Seizing the moment, Kris turned the sign to "Closed" and locked the front door. "It's Friday, and we worked like dogs this week. Enjoy a little head-start to your weekend." It wasn't hard to convince Marie to leave early, which gave Kris more time to prepare for her date.

It had taken some serious planning, but she knew what she wanted to do. A friend in Toronto had told her about a similar evening and Kris looked forward to trying it. She was still learning her way around Calgary, so she double checked her GPS to make sure her route for the evening was programmed correctly.

She picked Rudy up at his warehouse. "I'm ready," he said as he climbed into the passenger seat. "Where are we going? You wouldn't say."

Kris revved the engine. "Everywhere," she said, using the most mysterious voice she could.

When Rudy said it would be easy for her to find things to do, she started looking in earnest. There was always an event back home; she didn't know why she thought Calgary would be any different. Once she started searching, a whole new world opened to her. Tonight, she intended to share what she'd learned, and see how much of it Rudy already knew.

"Have you heard of a progressive dinner?" she asked.

"It's when couples go from house to house for each course."

"Right. We're doing that, but we're hitting different places for the appetizers, entrees, and desserts." She'd plotted out a course to cover as much of the city as she could. To make sure she included restaurants Rudy would like, she'd enlisted Tucker for help. If Rudy could recruit her assistant, she figured turnabout was fair play.

Their first stop was a vegetarian restaurant that reviews said had the best baked potato soup in the province. Rudy opted for minestrone. They both unzipped their coats in the car as she pulled out of the parking lot.

"Great soup. What's next?"

"Jingle Bell Way. It's only a slight detour." Kris was shocked to learn how seriously Calgarians took their outdoor Christmas decorating. Entire streets got together to plan; some of them even piped carols over exterior speakers. Visitors were encouraged to drive slowly down the street to view the displays and enjoy the music.

The people on the west side of the city had organized a breathtaking display. Although she only opened the windows a crack because of the cold, the faint music was more than enough to set the tone.

The LED lights weren't blindingly bright, but the way they reflected off the white snow seemed to double their effect. Some houses were all white, some all blue. One had bulbs that changed colours in time with the songs. They were all gorgeous.

Kris stopped the car to let a bunch of sightseers cross the street in front of her. "Hey, check it out!" The house on the corner had an inflatable poutine truck, with one elf working and one elf standing beside it enjoying a tray of fries, cheese curds, and gravy.

"That jumpstarted my Christmas spirit," Rudy said once they were back on the road. "I'm not sure if I should tell my mom to take a drive through there, though. It might give her ideas, and I'll be the one up on the ladder."

The next restaurant was only a few blocks away, so Kris parked before contributing to the conversation. "I'm glad my aunt only has lawn decorations. All we have to do is anchor them and run an extension cord. Although, she does own a dozen of them. She has a thing for cartoon characters in Santa hats. I think I've convinced her to go a more traditional route for the bakery, but she's recruited some friends, and I'm scared. They're decorating the place on Sunday. I'll have to wait and see what they did when I arrive on Monday."

Part of her looked forward to it; the other half was a little afraid. Her aunt was obsessed with garland. Kris pictured it on every window, every display case, and around the cash register. Luckily, Vivian kept it out of the back room for sanitary reasons.

"What is this place?" Rudy asked. She'd pulled in behind a building, denying him a chance to see the sign above the door.

"Italian. Marie recommended it. Specifically, she told me to get the lasagna or the ravioli. I'll look at the menu, but I admit I've been craving pasta all day."

"Me, too," Rudy said. Then he chuckled. "Now I know why Tucker raved about the spaghetti and Bolognese sauce he had for lunch. To get the idea into my head."

Kris whistled innocently.

"Is there something you'd like to share?"

Unlike him, she didn't intend to get busted for using his assistant as an informant. "I'll share whatever I order with you," she said.

He pulled the brim of her toque over her eyes. "Come on. The soup has worn off and I'm starving."

Kris took Marie's advice and ordered the ravioli. It was butternut squash, not meat, and came with a tomato sauce heavy on the basil. She loved it. Rudy got a piece of lasagna so big he couldn't finish it.

"Please tell me we are spending the rest of our evening on the sofa. I can't move. The garlic bread..." Rudy adjusted the collar of his coat to block the slight breeze that had come up.

She nodded in understanding. The garlic bread had been sublime. "Sorry to disappoint you, but sofas are not on the schedule. We'll have to hurry as it is." She hustled them back to the car. Although she had reservations for the restaurant where they were having dessert, they had one stop to make first.

"Where are we going?"

"I know you enjoy music, what with the Arrowhead concert you don't have a date for, so I thought you'd enjoy some Christmas carols."

Marie's younger sister was still in high school. Her band was holding a fundraising concert, and Kris had purchased two tickets to be supportive. She and Rudy wouldn't be able to stay for the whole thing, but according to the program, the event was broken into three acts.

They slipped into their seats during the second inter-mission.

Kris leaned closer when Rudy wrapped his arm around her shoulder. "Did you know I played in my high school band? Trumpet," he whispered.

She turned her head to stare at him. "No way! I did to. I still play." She'd begun to look for somewhere to play while she was in Calgary but finding a community band was proving to be impossible.

The kids were alright. They did a spectacular version of "Little Drummer Boy" with the school chorus. They snuck out the door as the last notes sounded. "We have just enough time to make our reservation," Kris said.

Rudy waited till they were in the car. "Trumpet, huh? What else don't I know about you?"

Kris thought for a moment. "I was part of a running group back home, but that's more of a spring-summer-fall thing. Especially here. Treadmills aren't the same. And the hills! We don't have hills in Toronto that are out to kill you."

He laughed at her, and she deserved it, but he didn't comment further on her lament for flat land. "Do you do marathons?"

She shook her head. "No, I save my competitive streak for dodgeball. Running is to get me outside and moving after being in a kitchen all day. How about you? What do you do for fun?"

"Dodgeball. Skiing, now that I'm back in Calgary. Cross-country and downhill, but more cross-country out of the city. I also take a lot of trips. I travel for work, but whenever I have vacation days, I try to get away. Usually somewhere warm," he added with a laugh.

"I can understand that." She'd managed a handful of trips to Jamaica to visit family since she'd graduated high school. She was lucky she only had to cover the plane fare since she always had a place to stay. She'd do it more often if she could.

She pulled into a strip mall off the northwest Crow Child Trail. There was a vacuum store, an investment office, and a dessert café that served the best pie in the city. Kris was confident in her baking skills, but when it came to somebody who spent all day, every day making pie, she didn't try to compete. "Are you ready for dessert?"

Rudy's stomach rumbled in response. "Do they have rhubarb?"

"They have it all."

The whole night had been wonderful, right down to Rudy asking for his ice cream on the side and then offering her the bowl, because he didn't want to "take away from the perfection of the pie." If Kris had any regrets for the evening, it was that she hadn't seen Rudy in this light while they'd known each other in Toronto.

"I'm sorry we have to end so early. My work days start at four o'clock in the morning." Nine at night for her was the equivalent for most people staying out till midnight.

"I don't mind at all. How could I, when we have such a good time together?"

They set down their forks in a comfortable silence. They had learned a lot about each other, and she was in no hurry for the night to be over. From the smile on his face, neither was Rudy. Finally, he spoke. "Are we on for a third date? Because I have an idea."

"I'm game if you are."

8. RUDY

SANTA CLAUS WAS a mysterious man indeed. He not only stayed out of sight on Christmas Eve, he was hard to find the other three-hundred-and-sixty-four days of the year too. Case in point, Rudy was on his second page of actors for hire who wore the infamous red suit in December, and none of them wanted anything to do with him.

"Sorry, buddy," his most recent St. Nick said. "I'm booked a year in advance. I have a couple dates left next November, but my schedule is full between now and New Year's."

"Thanks anyway." Rudy hit the "end call" button with more force than was necessary as his last chance disappeared into thin air.

He was stuck. Painfully stuck, since he was the one who'd promised—no, guaranteed—Santa would make an appearance at the party. There had to be something he hadn't thought of. At this point he was willing to fly somebody in from Vancouver. He would have said Edmonton, but he'd already called all those holly, jolly impersonators as well.

I suppose I could do it myself. The thought came unbidden into his brain. It had to be easier to buy or rent a Santa suit than it was to find somebody to fill it. Or, if he had his own suit, he could hire somebody to wear it.

He hadn't begun his search for costume rental companies before he was interrupted by a phone call.

"Rudy, this is John Tinder in December. Why haven't you responded to my email?"

Rudy gulped. The senior manager of mergers and acquisitions had a reputation of not suffering fools lightly. "Mr. Tinder, my email isn't open. Yet," he added as he clicked the icon.

Rudy had to read it twice. "Totally Iced agreed to participate in the 12 Sales of Christmas promotion. When did that happen?" He'd promised not to push Kris on business matters after making the initial overture, but surely, she would have mentioned going ahead with the contract.

"Yesterday. I need you to get to the bakery and get the paperwork signed today. The timing is already tight on this, and we need to have them locked in."

"Yes, sir. I'll head right over." He warned Tucker he'd be gone for the rest of the morning and hustled out the door with the papers hot off the printer.

They were definitely warmer than the reception he got at Totally Iced. He'd debated stopping for flowers and went with the impulse. Rudy burst through the door, bouquet in one hand, contract in the other, and congratulated Kris on taking the plunge.

To which she replied, "Are you crazy?"

"What? I was told—head office told me—Totally Iced was on board."

"Well, we're not. I spoke to my aunt like I said I would

but she didn't say anything about coming a decision. You promised me no pressure." The friendly look in her eyes from when she first spotted him had burned off in the fire he saw now. She was not pleased with him.

"It's not my fault," Rudy protested.

"I told you Marie and I couldn't possibly handle this order on such short notice." The bell over the front door jingled but neither of them looked up. "Who said we were going to do this? I'd like to talk to them."

"I did." Their attention turned to the woman standing at the front door. Vivian Singleton, holding a briefcase, frowned at her niece and smiled at him. "Mr. Gillespie, we'd be pleased to sign that contract."

"Excuse me?" they both said to the newcomer at the same time.

"Mr. John Tinder at North Pole Unlimited contacted me. We discussed renewing our contract and the new promotion, and I said we would participate."

"Aunt Vivian!"

"Perhaps I should excuse myself from this conversation," Rudy offered. He didn't want to step into the middle of a family spat.

"That's not necessary, Rudy."

He handed the contract to Vivian. "Please don't shoot the messenger," he said.

Vivian set her briefcase on the floor. "I'm sorry you found out like this, Kris. I was on my way over to discuss it with you. First of all, I saw my doctor yesterday. He said I can come back to work part-time."

"That's wonderful!"

It was. Rudy knew how worried Kris had been about her aunt, even while she said all the comforting phrases about her recovery. He was glad, too. He liked Vivian.

"Obviously, I can't return to the manager position yet, even if you do let me sit at your desk when I come to visit."

"It's still your desk. I'm just here temporarily."

"That's another thing. If I come back part-time, and I bring in a couple other part-time people to concentrate strictly on the North Pole Unlimited order, I know we can knock it out by the end of the month."

From the look on Kris's face, Rudy knew she thought her aunt's plans were optimistic at best. But it wasn't his place to say anything. His job was to return to the office with a signed contract or face the wrath of Mr. Tinder. Or worse, Jilly Lewis.

Kris made her argument anyway. "But we still have to hire people and order supplies. All of that takes time we don't have."

"I've already made some calls. I had student applications on file. My two top picks will be starting with me tomorrow."

"I guess that's settled then."

"Kris, dear, don't worry. It'll be fine. It'll be better than fine, it'll be fantastic!" Vivian promised. "Excuse me for a moment, Rudy. I'll run into the office to find a pen so I can get these signed right away."

She disappeared, Marie was still in the back, and all of a sudden, he was alone with Kris. "I'm sorry. I had no idea any of this was going on."

"Me, neither. I'm sorry, too. I know it wasn't your fault. I didn't expect this at all. She wasn't supposed to come back till the new year."

He heard the worry return to her voice. "Trust her to know how much she can do," he said. "I don't think she wants to relapse any more than you do."

"I know." But she didn't sound convinced.

Rudy handed her the flowers. They weren't much, but they were all he had. "I'll let you two talk." He'd intended to ask Kris out on their third date while he was there, kind of a double celebration, but now she had more important things on her mind.

For her, he'd wait.

INTERLUDE

NORTH POLE UNLIMITED HEADQUARTERS,
December, Manitoba

"Last week, we finalized the participants of the "12 Sales of Christmas" campaign," Nick Klassen announced at the staff meeting. The boardroom table was crowded with laptops and plates of sandwiches since they were gathered over their lunch hours.

The closer they got to Christmas, the more often the meetings. They also ran shorter; nobody could afford to be out of their office for long. "We'll be announcing them on the website soon, but Ginger is giving us a sneak peek at the new promotional material." Nick rose to his full height and reached behind his chair to turn out the light. The television on the wall sprang to life, and the North Pole Unlimited website appeared.

A tall redhead stood. "This will be going live tomorrow and will run for two weeks until the sales start. I want to thank everyone involved in getting this year's participants signed to the campaign. We have a terrific line-up, and they are all past catalogue favourites. We think our customers will love the variety." She raised a remote control. "Now let's get on with the show."

A pop-up window appeared in the middle of the screen. A familiar melody played faintly in the background. Digital snowflakes fluttered across the screen, turning into text that read, "For the 1st Sale of Christmas, my true love gave to me: A Dozen Chocolate Meringues from Totally Iced Bakery. Limited Quantities." More images flashed, displaying other products that would be available. At the bottom of it all, a small "Order Here" button flashed in the corner.

"I thought Totally Iced hadn't signed with us." Jilly's brown eyes glowered with suspicion.

"It's real. Apparently, Rudy is very convincing. He and John talked Vivian Singleton into it. John also added a signing bonus nobody could refuse," Nick said. He had authorized it, if only to arrange a Christmas present for Jilly.

"How limited of a sales run?" she asked.

Ginger handled that question. "I don't have the numbers on hand. The amounts vary by product. I think Totally Iced promised us four hundred units," she said.

"Will you excuse me for a minute?" Jilly asked. She left the room without waiting for a reply.

"I thought she'd be pleased. She's been calling me every day about Totally Iced," Graham said. The man mopped his face with a handkerchief. "I owe John and Rudy a thank-you. Maybe fruit-baskets. Your executive assistant was getting a little intense about those chocolate meringues."

Jilly returned ten minutes later, full of smiles and

utterly agreeable. She didn't even complain when a last-minute glitch left her in charge of updating payroll.

On the way out of the meeting, Nick fell into step beside her. When she followed him into his office, and the stuffed bass with the motion sensor on the wall greeted them, he let his curiosity show. "What was that about?"

"What?"

He swore she did it on purpose to drive him crazy. "You disappeared halfway through the meeting," Nick specified, running his fingers through his blond hair.

"I had to do a couple things."

"In the middle of the meeting?"

"They were important."

He sighed. "Do you want to elaborate?"

"Not really."

She'd definitely learned her evasion tactics from her former boss, his grandmother. "Elaborate," he ordered.

"I ordered a fruit basket for John as a thank you for getting Totally Iced back on board."

"That's only one thing."

Jilly groaned. "Fine. If you must know, I called the I.T. Department and had them add my Totally Iced order before the sale was advertised to the public."

"Was that necessary?"

"You obviously haven't had their chocolate meringues," she said haughtily. "I'm just glad they're back before I had to do something really drastic."

It took Nick a few seconds to fully process her last comment. After working with her for three years, he knew he had to carefully consider every word out of her mouth. "Did you already do something mildly drastic?"

She patted his arm. It would have comforted him, if he didn't feel her shaking with restrained laughter at the same time. "Nothing they can prove in court. Completely unrelatedly, don't worry if any odd invoices come in over the next couple weeks. I'll take care of them."

It was like she enjoyed torturing him. "That does not reassure me, Jilly."

9. RUDY

AN "ALL CLEAR" message waited for him back at his office. Vivian Singleton had called to let him know the contract was signed and ready to be picked up at his convenience, and that production was immediately. Rudy decided to give them at least a day to ensure she and Kris had things under control before he showed his face again.

Tucker had been his normal, efficient self while he was out, clearing Rudy's calendar until an eleven o'clock conference call. As if it knew he had a minute to himself, his phone rang.

"Rudy? It's Jennifer Chang. Can you talk for a minute? This is too involved to do over texts," she said in a rush.

Jennifer never sounded frazzled. Her cool head was the reason the Christmas party board was as organized as it was. "Of course."

"I got a series of requests from Cynthia for payments for a variety of entertainment expenses for the party. I'm sending you copies."

"Okay." He didn't hear a problem so far. If Cynthia needed supplies for her events, she should be reimbursed.

"No, not okay. Can you see them?"

"One second. Let me open the email."

"Can you believe this? We have a four-piece string quartet, an interior decorating firm, and a petting zoo. A freaking petting zoo, Rudy. What was she thinking?"

He burst out laughing and was met with silence at the other end of the line. Then Jennifer started laughing too. "I know, right?" she continued. "Cynthia insists she has your support with this, and with Warren gone, a majority is three people. I wanted to confirm these ideas were a hard no from you."

"No, double no, and probably still no. Although I'd consider the petting zoo if I knew more about it and if it wasn't in December in Calgary."

She laughed again. "I'll let her know her requests were declined. If you get an irate call from Cynthia, you'll know why. Have fun!"

It didn't take long. Cynthia leapt right into complaining. "I thought, with our history, we'd be on the same team, Rudy. I'm trying to elevate this party, but you're all working against me. Do you know how lucky we'd be to sign the Chamber String Quartet? The two weddings I did in the fall raved about them."

He thought about reminding her that their history consisted of a single date, but he didn't want to have that conversation any more than he wanted to have their current one. "Cynthia, it's a party *for children*. We don't need musicians. We're already having a Santa Sing-along."

He heard her huff into the receiver. "And what was wrong with the decorator?"

"Why would we need one? We're in the community centre."

"Rudy, Clarice and Tim are the premier designers in the city. They're offering a dozen themed Christmas trees to decorate the room."

Those didn't sound terrible. Ornament- and tinsel-laden trees sounded a lot prettier than garland taped to walls and snowflakes hung from the ceiling. "How much was that?"

"Only a hundred dollars a tree."

"No. That's a huge chunk of the budget for some sparkle."

"Are you saying kids don't like sparkles?"

He should have stayed at Totally Iced and immersed himself in the family drama there. "Kids love sparkles, but not at the cost of half the gift budget. What about the petting zoo?"

"Children like animals. Not that I'd get anywhere near the mangy beasts. But they're expecting their deposit today, and I don't have time to cancel it."

Of course, she didn't. "I'll take care of it," Rudy said. He'd do anything to end this conversation.

"Fine. Since you and Jennifer vetoed all my ideas, I'll have to find something new. Again."

"Cynthia, you know we'd all be happy to help you."

"I'm perfectly capable of selecting entertainment. Now if you'll excuse me, I'll get back to work."

Rudy searched the petting zoo website in hopes there was a way to cancel a booking online. He got as far as the homepage before an ad caught his eye. "That can't be right," he said to himself before he read it again. It didn't change. "Rent a Rudolph for Christmas."

Having reindeer at the party would be cool. It would

be like Santa's sleigh was parked right outside. The kids would get a kick out of it. So would he.

A few clicks and a phone call later, he was back on the phone with Jennifer. The petting zoo Cynthia had found was willing to rent them two reindeer—with antlers —for an hour. They'd construct a temporary stall in the community centre parking lot and provide food and clean-up.

It wasn't a done deal by any means, but the online photos charmed Rudy so much, he told Jennifer he was willing to pay for it out of his own pocket. He *needed* Dasher and Dancer at the party, now that he knew it was an option. Jennifer okayed his proposal, and he called Kris to tell her about the party's latest additions to the guest list, but she distracted him.

"This North Pole Unlimited thing with Aunt Vivian is settled. If it works out like she's planned, it won't impact my work schedule at all. I don't know what you had in mind, but I might be able to do our third date this week-end, if you're still interested."

The good news just kept coming. "I am. Does Friday night work for you?" He knew exactly what he wanted to do.

10. KRIS

VIVIAN SINGLETON HAD a lot of sayings like, "when in doubt, open a new package of baking powder" and "always add more chocolate chips." Kris's favourite was, "those cookies won't bake themselves."

Her aunt and her two new helpers were working on the meringues, and Kris and Marie had to make everything else to keep the bakery's shelves stocked and orders filled.

Kris didn't mind the work. The hard part was knowing she'd be too busy to keep an eye on Vivian. It was terrific that her aunt was well enough to return to work; Kris knew how much she missed the bakery. Not just the baking, but the camaraderie and the clients. But Vivian was coming back to a load of stress and hard work —even if it was only half time. As much as she loved her job, Kris didn't want her to suffer a setback.

A smaller part of her acknowledged that she had proprietary feelings over a shop that wasn't hers. She wanted Aunt Vivian to check with her before making big decisions for the bakery. Her aunt may own it, but Kris had been running it for months. She needed to get that under control. But her aunt was right. Contracts were her decision, and Kris would have to go along with whatever she decided.

Ordering the meringue ingredients was the easy part. The previous afternoon, right after Vivian dropped her NPU contract bomb, Kris had contacted her supplier and requested enough supplies to make four hundred dozen cookies. She tried to wrap her head around the idea of four thousand, eight hundred chocolate meringues, but her brain couldn't handle it.

Marie froze at the news. "How many? We don't have to make them, do we?" she repeated more than once.

"Nope, it will all fall on Aunt Vivian and her two new assistants," Kris assured her. "Let's make some space for them." The trio would be working from open to close on the specialty treats. It was easier to give them a dedicated work area and ovens than compete for counter space. She and Marie spent an extra hour organizing the already crowded kitchen and finagled a compromised which would leave both teams slightly squished but able to work.

The day after that, the bakery was fuller than it had ever been. At seven o'clock sharp, Vivian introduced her two new assistants. "Kris, Marie, I'd like you to meet Pat One and Pat Two. They're both from the culinary arts program at the college."

Pat One introduced herself as Patricia Brown. She looked much younger than Kris remembered being when she was in college. Everything about the woman was over-poweringly vanilla. Her hair was back but styled to a point where a hair net would barely contain it. Her flawless make-up would run the second she got near a hot oven, and her clothes were perfectly correct but looked like they came from a boutique. She was dressed for a photo shoot of a bakery, not for actually doing any labour in one.

That was nothing compared to the problems Kris had with Pat Two. He was ready to work and wore a ready, welcoming smile. But Kris froze at his introduction. "Hi, I'm Pat Quinn. I think you know my sister, Cynthia."

It took her a moment to break through the shock. Without knowing a single other thing about the young man, Kris was prepared to dislike him. Kris stared at Pat Two. She didn't see any resemblance to her nemesis on the Christmas party committee. She shook his outstretched hand. "Hi, yes, I know Cynthia. Welcome to Totally Iced. I'll let you get baking."

In between batches of sugar cookies, Kris watched her aunt organize Pat One and Pat Two and demonstrate the chocolate meringue recipe. Pat Two, Patrick, asked a lot of questions. Pat One looked bored at Vivian's insistence they follow the "easy" recipe to the letter.

"Trust her to know her limits," Kris whispered to herself, echoing Rudy's advice. Hovering over her aunt out of concern would not only undermine her in front of the new employees, but was also guaranteed to annoy Aunt Vivian. Kris kept her eyes on her own work.

At noon, when Kris was about to remind her aunt that part-time meant just that, Vivian approached her. "Can you believe that we're ready to start packing already?"

"You are?" It might only be the first batch out of dozens, but it was a start that gave Kris hope.

"Yes, isn't that fantastic? Thank goodness I forgot to cancel the order with the Christmas shipping supplies. Where did you put them all?"

"In the storage room."

"Excellent. I'll call in the Pats to help me get them out and organized."

As soon as her aunt was out of sight, Marie whacked her in the arm. "Are you crazy?"

Kris rubbed her biceps where the wooden spoon had left a greasy imprint. "What now?"

"You can't let Vivian into the storage room, or did you forget what we hid at the bottom of the pile?"

It took Kris a minute to remember. "We can't let her go in there!" She raced out of the kitchen. "Aunt Vivian, don't you dare lift any of those boxes. I'll get them for you!"

The next day got off to a rough start for Vivian and Pat Two when Pat One was an hour late. "I overslept," was her only excuse.

Kris was on her way to the storage room for another container of molasses when she stopped beside the mixer. "Stop," she told Pat One before the young woman hit the power button.

"What's wrong over there?" her aunt asked.

"Small mistake. Pat One added two tablespoons of cream of tartar instead of two teaspoons." It was easy enough to do. Kris had made the same mistake on countless recipes.

"No, I didn't," Pat One protested.

"It's okay, everyone does it. At least we caught it before you added the sugar." The egg whites would be a loss, but it was better than losing both eggs and sugar.

"I didn't make a mistake!"

When Vivian came over, Kris stepped aside. This was her aunt's team; she could deal with it. Kris already had gingerbread on her mind. Now, with the thought of all those egg whites, she began thinking of recipes that used a lot of yolks.

Kris ignored the grumbling as Pat One poured the mixture in the trash, washed the bowl, and began measuring again. Before she knew it, it was noon and her aunt was heading out. "Please keep an eye on the Pats. They have another batch to go this afternoon, and then they'll be packaging for the rest of the day. Right on schedule."

Kris walked her to the office to get her coat. "I was concerned when North Pole Unlimited didn't renew their order after the last holiday season," her aunt continued. "It's good to know it was an oversight and not a quality control issue. I hope next year we'll be back in the regular catalogue, but even this one-day sale will keep us fresh in their customers' minds. It's substantial work, but the payoff is worth it."

"If the way they chased you down for the contract is any indication, you have nothing to worry about next year." Not that she would be around to see it. She'd agreed to stay on until her aunt was back on her feet, and Vivian hadn't asked her to stay longer. At first, Kris didn't mind the temporary gig. Now, she regretted not insisting on being permanent, or at least long-term, from the beginning. Calgary was growing on her in numerous ways, from the job to the landscape to her social life. Especially when it came to her social life.

"That's a whole year away. Let's get through this. I'll have a nap this afternoon and come back fresh tomorrow."

"I like that plan. I can keep an eye on them for the rest of the day." After several batches already, they should know what they were doing. Packaging was the easy part.

It turned out she didn't need to watch both Pats all

day. About fifteen minutes after Vivian left, Pat One threw in her apron. "I quit."

"What?"

"I didn't think it would be like this. I thought I'd be decorating cakes and icing cookies. This is all grunt work."

"Well, yeah, you were hired to complete a single order of the same cookie. Once that's done, you get to work on other stuff, more fun stuff. You don't start off doing wedding cakes."

"I should. I was first in my class for my sugar skills and my piping technique. This is boring."

Kris had had this same conversation on her first job. Luckily, she had it with a friend who'd talked some sense into her; she hadn't complained directly to the boss. "I get that, but everybody starts at the bottom. You were specifically hired for a cookie contract. It's not glamorous, but you're doing a good job."

"I can get a better job. I'm out of here."

Then she left.

"This can't be happening," Kris whispered to herself. They needed Pat One. At least, they needed her hands. "Aunt Vivian is going to kill me."

"It's not your fault. This isn't the first placement she's walked out on," Pat Two said.

"How about you? Are you sticking around?"

"If you're willing to keep me, I'll keep making cookies. I think I've been doing okay so far."

"More than okay. Please don't quit. We need you."

"Then I'll take the last trays out of the oven and start packaging. Vivian showed me how yesterday."

"Fantastic." Kris didn't understand how Pat Two could be related to Cynthia. He was friendly and helpful and competent at the tasks assigned to him. She wanted two of him.

Vivian was understandably upset the next morning. "I checked all her references. She looked good on paper."

"It happens, Aunt Viv. Totally Iced was simply not a good fit for her. Do you have anyone else in your files? Anybody who wants a last-minute job before Christmas?"

"Not that I can think of, but I'll try, sweetie."

But there was nobody. No recent graduates looking for work. No students. No semi-retired bakers who wanted to get back in the game for a couple weeks to earn some extra cash before the holidays. All her calls—and Kris's—went unanswered.

Vivian and Pat Two worked all morning. Her aunt insisted she was fine to keep going, but when Kris caught her leaning against the doorframe to the storage room trying to catch her breath, Kris overrode her protests. "Home, bed, nap. Pat Two and Marie and I can do this. Our in-house customers will happily deal with a few days of chocolate meringues being the special."

Wednesday was a disaster as they tried to find a new rhythm. They eventually got the cookie timing perfected but the three of them were there until eight o'clock packaging a dozen treats at a time. They were so far behind schedule, Kris mentally waved her weekend good-bye.

Then Thursday happened.

Pat Two had shared an idea the day before—premeasuring the meringues' ingredients and having them ready to pour. Seizing the idea to save even a few minutes, Kris did the same to prepare the bakery's regular recipes. "Pat Two, you're a genius." They hit their daily goal and made up some of their shortfall from earlier in the week. It was enough to give Kris hope for the weekend. She'd still be working, but she might be able to squeeze in a couple hours for a personal life.

"Call him," her aunt said.

"Who?"

"Rudy, of course. Weren't you supposed to have a third date this weekend?"

"Yes, but I still have a ton of work left to do."

"The cookies will wait. You need to take a break before you sacrifice your health like I did. Put sugar and eggs out of your mind for a while. You're young. Act like it."

"I'm twenty-eight."

Her aunt levelled a glare on her that lacked its usual fire. Kris laughed. "Fine, I'll call Rudy to give him an update, but he'll have to do the asking." She'd apologized for flipping out on him when he brought over the contract, but that was the last real conversation they'd shared.

When Vivian bustled her into the office and closed the door, Kris ran out of excuses. She took a deep breath and began to type. "*Hey, can you talk?*" she texted.

"*To you, always.*"

"*NPU cookies finally under control.*"

"*Working this weekend?*"

"*Yes, but not Friday night.*"

"*Date night?*"

"*If you want.*"

"*I WANT. Will text you the details.*" Then he added a red rose emoji.

When Kris emerged smiling, she saw a weight lift from her aunt's shoulders. "I assume he asked you out."

"Friday night. Details forthcoming. To me, not you," Kris added.

"I'm not offended. Marie will fill me in," her aunt teased.

She laughed because it was true. "Don't you have cookies to make?"

Friday didn't go quite as smoothly. Kris opened the doors to two delivery trucks. She didn't mind the first, which was a flower arrangement from Rudy. The card read "Looking forward to tonight."

She whipped out her phone and took a selfie with the bouquet. She sent the image and a short message. "Beautiful!"

When he responded with "So are the flowers," her heart melted. The work day couldn't end soon enough.

The second package was much less welcome. It contained a variety of paper plates, bags of biodegradable cutlery, and assorted napkins, all with different Christmas themes. "This is ridiculous," Kris complained to Marie. "I didn't order any of these. I don't even recognize the company name. There's got to be two hundred dollars' worth of product here. I absolutely do not have time for this."

Nevertheless, she called the company. Kris assumed people would want to have a massive box of misdirected goods returned if they weren't paid for, but it wasn't that easy. "You've received our standard corporate trial pack," the customer service operator said. "The variety of plates and napkins are complimentary when samples are requested."

"But I didn't request a sample pack," Kris repeated.

"I don't know what to say to that." She heard clicking in the background as the representative asked her to wait while she searched for Kris's name again. "I think you're right. The order is addressed to Kris Kringleton but didn't come from Totally Iced. But since it's unlikely we'll receive the returned shipment before the end of the season, it's not worth to ship it back. Please keep it, with our compliments."

Kris couldn't argue with free. But she did growl about losing more storage room. "At least some of the shipping boxes are gone now," Marie said in commiseration as they reorganized the closet yet again, keeping the costumes buried at the bottom. "Try not to think about it when you're on your date with Rudy."

"I'm pretty sure it'll be the furthest thing from my mind."

11. RUDY

LIKE THE DATE KRIS PLANNED, his didn't require fancy clothes. Rudy had recommended she dress warmly, so when he arrived at the bakery, he was pleased to see her in heavy jeans, thick boots, and a monstrously long, cherry-red scarf over her parka.

"I know you've been crazy busy this week, so I've planned a fun but short evening."

"How did you know how busy I've—" Kris halted herself mid-question. "You have spies everywhere. Thank you. I'm excited to go out, but I'll appreciate the early night."

"My spies also said you had a particular fondness for hot chocolate from the Coffee Run truck. I know where they're going to be."

Kris gave a fist pump.

If he'd had any warning the temperature planned to drop to twenty below, he would have changed his plans. Rudy slapped his hands together to get the blood flowing. The thick leather mittens made a muffled whump, but the fleece inside rubbed warmly against his fingers. He was glad Kris hadn't backed out of their date under the stars. Of course, most people pictured a walk along a sandy beach when they heard that description. It was a little different when it was December in Canada.

Olympic Plaza was in the heart of downtown Calgary. In the summer, it was a gorgeous green space with a pretty reflecting pond, where business people took outdoor breaks over lunch and visitors could enjoy the park all day long. In the winter, the city let the pond freeze into a huge, outdoor skating rink. It was crowded from opening to close. The daytime skaters enjoyed sunshine and blue skies over the white rink. The evening visitors had the city skyline and Christmas decorations to light up the night.

Rudy thought she'd be more excited than nervous, until he discovered why she was so quiet. "I know you don't ski, but what do you mean, you don't skate? Do you know how?" He gave her gloved hand a squeeze as they stood in line for rental skates.

"In theory. I haven't been on skates since..." Kris paused to think about it. "Since elementary school. You may have to hold me to keep me upright."

They found an open bench and pulled off their boots. Kris yanked on the laces and tied the white leather tightly around her ankles. Rudy did the same to his black ones. Kris wobbled for a few steps on the outdoor carpeting until she made it to the ice. She balanced carefully while she sent him on a lap around the rink to warm up. "One of us has to be in skating shape or we'll both be in trouble," she joked.

She was right. Her feet almost went out from under her the second she took her first step, but he had a firm grip on her biceps. She took another step, and again he was the only reason she didn't hit the ground. "Perhaps this wasn't the best idea," he murmured. They were supposed to be having fun, not trying to avoid serious injury.

Kris shook her head. "Nope." A puff of air came out of her mouth like a cloud. "I can't quit on my first try. Let's do it again, slow and steady."

Rudy waited till she had both skates firmly on the ice. Then he turned and began skating backward slowly, towing her around the rink. Kris didn't even move her feet. Her entire job consisted of not falling down. She grinned when they completed their first circuit. Doing that one thing had taken all her concentration; she looked exhausted, but adorably pleased with herself.

He could have suggested they end the date there, but her proud smile made him reconsider. "Look at you!" he said. "I think you earned a hot chocolate and a break before we go again."

"That sounds perfect."

Rudy pulled her to a bench on the edge of the ice. "I'll be right back." He kept an eye on her while he waited to give his order at the food truck. Now he had another hobby to add to the list of things he knew about her. Kris liked to people-watch. She looked perfectly content checking out the rest of the skaters: a pair who knew what they were doing spun and pirouetted in the middle, little rookie skaters wobbled by with hockey helmets on, and several couples glided by slowly, hand in hand.

He looked twice at the cinnamon buns but decided to save them for their second cup of cocoa. If they were outside for any length of time, they'd need one. As he carefully carried the cups back to Kris, he noticed Cynthia Quinn approaching her from the other side. The brunette wore a spotless white parka, with a matching white scarf and hat.

He was close enough to hear the conversation, but a mob of mini future hockey stars blocked his path. Rudy heard Cynthia say, "Kris, I thought that was you. Let me introduce the caterer for the party on Saturday. Peter Watson, this is Kris Singleton. She's on the board with me."

A tall, skinny man stuck out his hand. "Pleased to meet you."

Rudy watched as Kris slowly made her way to her feet and balanced carefully while she shook his hand. "Pleased to meet you too, but what do you mean, Cynthia? Our caterer? We aren't having a caterer."

They'd had this discussion half a dozen times already: at the meetings, by text, through email. The menu was already set.

"I made an executive decision," Cynthia said dismissively. "I couldn't bear the thought of plates full of hotdogs and chips and unpeeled Mandarin oranges. What we have planned will be so much better." She plucked at the fake fur lining her mitten cuff. "I guarantee will be worth the cost."

Rudy began weaving through the children surrounding him, his patience expended as he listened to Cynthia try to bulldoze Kris into accepting an underhanded move as a done deal.

He should have known she could handle it by herself. "Mr. Watson, I'm afraid there has been a mistake. A terrible mistake."

The other man's attention bounced between the two women. "What's going on? Cynthia told me it was a Christmas party for two hundred. I'm willing to negotiate a good price since my business is new. We discussed starting with avocado gazpacho—"

"A children's Christmas party," Kris interrupted. "A "Jingle Bells, Batman smells" age kids party."

"Definitely no gazpacho then," he said.

"Peter, this is a minor misunderstanding. We definitely want the menu we discussed." Cynthia turned redder by the second. The contrast against her scarf made her look like a tomato. She turned to Kris. "You are humiliating me."

Rudy arrived and wrapped his arm around Kris's waist to show his support in every way she needed it. "I'm sorry you were misled, Mr. Watson. There is no catering contract."

"I'm sure we can come to some kind of understanding," Cynthia said quickly. "Can I speak to you for a moment, Rudy?"

Her friend was having none of it. "You planned that menu knowing the party was for children? Do you have any idea how inappropriate those dishes are? Four-year-olds and bruschetta with balsamic vinegar?" He shuddered. "It would destroy my reputation to misjudge my clients so badly. How could you suggest that? Are you even authorized to sign the contract?"

"No, she's not," Rudy said. "Contracts require board approval, and they run through Jennifer Chang, the chairperson."

"I thought I had your support, Rudy. I can't believe you're turning on me like this, just to support your new girlfriend!" Cynthia's tantrum was drawing a crowd, but he couldn't afford to show weakness. They could end up with Christmas clowns.

"And you," she continued, whirling on Peter. "I

offered you this chance because I thought we could work together in the future. I have dozens of weddings in my calendar. Dozens! Now I wouldn't work with you if you paid me, and don't even think of asking me for a referral for the Jameson party."

Finally, Cynthia turned on Kris. "Everybody—you especially—have undermined every idea I've had for the stupid Christmas party. Since I'm obviously a liability on the committee, I'll save us both problems in the future and resign right now."

"The party is in a week. You've put in too much work to quit now."

"No. You obviously think you're better off without me. I'm happy to oblige." She spun again, her coat flapping around her like a cape, and stormed away. Her exit would have been much more dramatic if she hadn't hit a patch of clear ice in the middle of the rink. Her arms flailed the windmills and her feet went in opposite directions. She caught herself in a crouch before her behind hit the ground. Rudy tried not to laugh as she slowly minced her way to the far edge.

Kris slapped his arm. "It's not funny."

"It was a little funny."

"Are you sure you were done with her before our first date? Because I don't think she got that memo."

"I was more than clear that our first date was our last. Don't let her get in your head," he warned. "After that, I doubt she'll be back."

"I almost hope she will be," Kris said to his shock. Then she continued. "Cynthia was the entertainment coordinator. There's no way she's going to tell us what she has organized. We'll have to make a whole new plan. In a week!"

"I'll handle it," Rudy said. Kris couldn't add another thing to her already overflowing plate. He barely got to see her as it was. If she had to perform Cynthia's duties in addition to the cookie contract, he might as well write off any chance of seeing her until the new year. "I already know some of what she was arranging. I can finish the job, no problem."

"There is one." Kris turned back to Peter Watson. "I'm sorry you got pulled into the middle of this. I don't know what your cancellation fees are—"

"It's okay." The sandy-haired man shook his head. "We literally signed the contract this afternoon, so it's not like I'm losing any business. Cynthia was right. My business is just starting, so my holiday calendar is empty. This project was supposed to get me some visibility in the city, but I don't think I'd get a lot of wedding bookings from a kids' party. No offense."

"None taken," Rudy said.

"But since we're talking, do you have any friends with weddings coming up? Or your own?" Peter asked.

"What?"

Peter waggled his hand at him and Kris. Rudy still had his arm around her waist. He hadn't noticed that she'd covered his hand with her own. Then Peter pointed at his head, and Rudy realized he and Kris were also wearing matching toques: his was navy with white trim, while hers was white with navy.

"No weddings here," he said. "This is our third date."

"Keep me in mind. You never know," Peter said. "Good luck with your party."

"Thanks, we'll need it."

Rudy guided Kris back to the bench, and they sipped

their hot chocolate in silence for a few moments. "How much trouble are we in with the party?" she asked.

"None."

"I do have—will have—the food under control. I know Jennifer has taken care of the location and decorations. You got all the corporate donations, and you already took care of buying the gifts after Warren bailed on us. But we're still looking for a Santa, and now the entertainment is falling through the cracks. It can't all fall on your shoulders."

"They're pretty wide shoulders. I've got this. If I hit any snags, I'll ask Jennifer for help."

"You can call me, too."

"You're even busier than I am. It'll be fine." He refused to let her worry about it. "Let's finish our cocoa and take another loop around the rink. One of us has an early bedtime, which works out great for me because I need to arrange a post-party and post-contract date that will be some place with central heating and a fireplace," Rudy said. He tapped the brim of her toque.

Having a couple extra hours to work on the party wouldn't hurt either.

12. KRIS

IT WAS THURSDAY. The last day of November, the second last day before the children's Christmas party, and Kris was totally whipped. But four hundred boxes of chocolate meringues were baked, packaged, and ready to be shipped. She and Marie slumped in the wire-frame chairs in front of the bakery windows, too tired to enjoy their coffees. At the table beside them, Kris's new seasonal hire looked just as exhausted. Aunt Vivian had left at noon, swearing she planned to sleep for a week, leaving Pat Two to finish the boxing by himself. "We did it, people. You were both amazing. North Pole Unlimited is sending a courier for these tomorrow, and they will be on their way to happy customers on the third of December," Kris said.

Forty-eight hundred cookies. The number blew Kris's mind, but they'd done it. Now it was back to the regular grind. After the last two weeks, it would feel like a vacation. "Who's looking forward to making anything other than meringues tomorrow?" she asked.

Three hands waved in the air, including her own.

"I'll even make fruitcake," Marie volunteered.

"I thought you didn't like it," Kris said.

"Like it? No. Stuff half the thing in my mouth in one sitting? Yes," Marie reminisced with a happy sigh. "It's too rich to eat every day, but it's my new favourite Christmas treat. I'd love the recipe."

Kris was confused, but she thought it was because she was so tired. "You know the recipe. You worked on the first batch."

"But I wasn't paying attention then because I didn't know how good it was! Please tell me we're making another batch."

Kris flopped her head to look at the calendar behind the cash register. It had their daily production schedule printed in her aunt's handwriting. "I can't tell you when we're doing it again off the top of my head. If you want to bring me the calendar, I'll look it up for you."

Marie twisted in her chair. "The calendar, which is all the way over there? I can wait till tomorrow."

"Everything can wait till tomorrow. Go home and relax," Kris ordered her staff. She planned to take her own advice. When she walked through the door to her tiny basement apartment, she briefly considered doing her laundry but decided it could wait a couple more days. She wanted a full night's sleep, even if she knew she'd dream of chocolate meringues.

Her bed, with its thick lilac duvet and squishy foam pillows, called to her. She was digging through her dresser drawer for pajamas when her phone rang. And rang and rang.

"You've got to be kidding me." She swiped it off the table and answered it with a gruff "Hello?"

"I forgot the activities!"

Kris had never heard Rudy panic before. She'd heard him complain and cajole and tease, but never panic. "What are you talking about?"

"For Saturday. I remembered the entertainment. I have a Santa suit. I booked the sound system and made copies of the song lyrics for the kids, so the singalong is set. Jennifer agreed I could do the reindeer rental, so I did. The presents are bought, wrapped, and labelled. You're handling the food. But I forgot to organize games and prizes for the kids. What are we going to do? The party is in two days!"

Kris reached for her coat. "We're going shopping. Do you know the Dollar and More Party Store by the airport?" She hadn't been to the Calgary location, but she'd memorized the layout to the one she used to visit in Toronto with her sister.

"I can find it. Will they have what we need to entertain two hundred children? I can't believe I was so concerned with Santa, I forgot."

"Bring your wallet. Jennifer can reimburse you. I'll see you there in an hour."

Kris concentrated so hard on the traffic that she was sitting in the parking lot waiting for him before she realized he said he had a Santa suit. What a relief! It was a smart move on his part—providing the suit and hiring an actor to fill it rather than try to find a professional Santa at the last minute.

Rudy ran to her car, his jacket unzipped and scarf flapping in the wind. "They close in an hour."

"That's plenty of time." She held his hand as they slipped across the icy ground. "Grab a cart and tell me about the reindeer." Because she hadn't heard anything about reindeer.

"Cynthia found a place that did a petting farm. I discovered they'll also bring two reindeer to your Christmas event so the kids can look at them. Jennifer thought it was a good idea, too, so we're having them in the parking lot. But that was easy. How are we going to keep them—the kids, not the reindeer—entertained for two hours?"

"I have some ideas." Kris had substituted at her sister's day care often enough to know what would appeal to the various age groups they'd be dealing with.

The store had aisles dedicated to children's birthday parties. She steered Rudy away from the holiday displays at the front and headed straight to the craft supplies. Her first move was to throw boxes of crayons into the cart. "We can get free images to colour from the internet and print them off. All we need are a few tables with a basket of crayons and a stack of papers. Instant quiet-down-space for kids after we get them all hyper," she explained at Rudy's confused face.

"Brilliant. I have a printer at the office. Can you send me some links?"

"No problem."

Rudy stood beside the cart, unmoving. "How are we getting them all hyper? We can't have a table full of candy. Even I know that."

Kris burst out laughing. "No, we can't give them candy, but we can give them prizes. Ready to pin a carrot on Frosty?"

She wasn't sure what the store had in stock, but if they couldn't pin a carrot on a snowman, they could tape a stocking on a fireplace or an ornament on a tree. Two plastic snowman shower curtains, six sheets of orange poster board, and a dozen rolls of tape later, they had their next game.

"One more, I think," Kris said. Rotating the kids through the games should only take an hour. When they added in time for snacks and songs and Santa, the afternoon would be gone.

"What do you have in mind?"

"Ice fishing."

Before she had a chance to explain, Rudy's face lit up. "I remember those prize fishing ponds from my school carnivals. You tie a clothespin on a fishing line and toss it behind a curtain. Then somebody clips a prize to it. We need some good prizes for that."

"Definitely. We'll need some stickers."

"Trading cards."

"Glow in the dark bracelets."

"Toy cars." Rudy laughed. "Man, children are easily amused."

Kris raised an eyebrow. "I bought myself a set of stickers for next year's work calendar." She made sure to grab an extra set of birthday ones for clients, so they could track when cakes were due. They were both practical and fun.

"I still have the toy corvette I got for my eighth birthday on my dresser," he admitted.

"Then find something to use for fishing poles, so we can continue the tradition." She loved that he didn't even question her. She sent him looking for supplies, not know if the store carried what they needed, but Rudy returned victorious. "I found a row with a bunch of stuff we can use for prizes!" he added, waving a handful of broom handles. Then he shoved his basket at her. It was heaped with cheap ornaments and glitter pens so winners could write their names on them, Christmas-themed cookie cutters, dinosaur figurines, mini colouring books, and sticker sheets.

They were on their way to the cash register when Kris stopped dead in the middle of the aisle. Rudy couldn't stop fast enough and rammed the cart into her. "I'm sorry, are you okay?"

"No, I'm an idiot." She pointed to the stand they'd hurried past when they first arrived. "I'm in charge of food and I totally forgot about serving it, but those won't do at all." The display was filled with silver snowflake-printed napkins and Rudolphs with sparkling red noses. "Who puts glitter on napkins? Who thought that was a good idea?" There were a handful of usable Santa plates, but the snowman ones were downright scary. Kris showed him a set. "Is it me, or does Frosty look like he's seen a ghost?" The snowman's eyes were comically big, and for some reason the artist had given him angled eyebrows which added to his shocked look.

"We can't serve food on those. We'll scare the kids," Rudy said in agreement.

She quickly scanned the rest of the aisle. "Ugh, there's nothing here I like. I suppose we could get plain red and green."

"Are you sure you don't already have that stuff?" Rudy asked.

"I'm sure. I never had a chance to go shopping."

He reached out to stop her from grabbing a stack of napkins. "Wait. I'm sure Marie told Tucker that someone sent you some stuff by mistake. I could have sworn she said something about plates and—"

"Yes. Yes, we did." How could she forget the massive box of paper products hiding in her storage closet? "We're saved!" Plus, she'd get her storage space back. It was a double win.

Kris helped Rudy load everything in to the back of his SUV. It filled it to the roof. "Do you happen to know if the community centre has a liquor license?"

"I don't think we can give the kids booze if we can't give them candy, Kris."

She snickered. "No, for us. Once the party is done, we're going to need it. Two hours to set up, two hours of pandemonium, and two hours to break everything down and clean the room. I had no idea six hours was so much work to organize. I can't believe Aunt Vivian has done it for the last ten years. The woman is amazing."

"She is. She and you and Jennifer are all invited to my office afterwards to celebrate another successful party. On Sunday. I think we'll need Saturday night to recover." He paused, then grinned. "We'll have it catered. Maybe we should call Peter."

"Don't joke. I'll hold you to that. For the last few nights I've been dreaming of gazpacho and I don't even know if I like it in real life."

She saw the snow whirling around them, but she didn't notice the cold when Rudy stood in front of her. "I wish I could ask you out for supper tonight, but I know you've been working double time for the last couple weeks, and I already interrupted your evening off."

Kris didn't mind. Her body was dead tired but the rest of her was energized from the time they spent together. "Do you want to grab a coffee?"

"Yes, but I want you to grab some rest more. Let's plan something for after the party. Something quiet and relaxing," he suggested. "You know what? I'll find something to make up for the ice skating."

"I liked the ice skating."

"I did, too but Cynthia spoiled the mood. We'll try again. Something just the two of us."

She was about to protest when a yawn broke free. She'd put in more hours than he knew, staying after Marie and Pat Two left for the night, trying to get a batch or two ahead of the North Pole Unlimited order. A quiet night at home, albeit with a late start, was exactly what the doctor ordered. "I'll hold you to that."

Rudy reached out. For a moment she thought he was going to kiss her, but instead he pulled her hood over her head. "Sleep well, Kris. I'll see you bright and early on Saturday."

It couldn't come soon enough.

13. RUDY

HE LOOKED AROUND to make sure nobody was watching, then gave a fist pump. The reindeer were even cooler than he imagined. The handler had even let him inside the fence to feed a carrot to the one they called Piper. The bigger-than-he-expected beast wasn't named after anyone on Santa's official sleigh team, but it was still cool.

Rudy had arrived two hours early to assist in the party preparations. Jennifer put him to work, unfolding tables and unstacking chairs for the lunch service. Kris was busy in one corner with another volunteer, setting up the first of the activities.

The games weren't time- or labour-intensive, but they would distract the kids for a few minutes, which was the intention. The previous iterations of the committee had structured a successful party plan, and this year's didn't intend to deviate from it.

He and Kris found themselves alone for a moment, all the other volunteers busy in different areas. "Is it weird that I think I'm more hyper than the kids will be?

Everyone is going to have such a good time," she whispered. She shook his arm excitedly. "By the way, the reindeer are brilliant. The kids will go insane when they see them. Then they have games and lunch and Santa and singing and presents." She gave his arm another squeeze. "They'll love it."

"They will." He glanced around the hall; everyone else was still occupied with other tasks. He bent so his lips were right at Kris's ear. "I'm definitely more eager for this party to start than the kids are. Of course, I already got my present."

Her eyes went wide. "You did?"

Rudy moved in a little more and dropped a quick kiss on her lips. She tasted like the candy cane she'd been nibbling all morning. "See? Early merry Christmas to me."

Her mouth made a surprised "Oh," but she recovered quickly. Then she grabbed his battery-operated, light-up Christmas tree tie and pulled him closer. "I want a Christmas present too," she whispered, just before she kissed him back.

"Hey, you two, find some mistletoe later. We still have work to do," Jennifer called from across the hall. "Don't you have serving tables to set up?"

"Grinch!" Kris hollered back, much to his amusement. She let go of his tie. "Sadly, she's right. We have lots left to do."

"Then we'll go on our date."

"I can't wait."

Kris disappeared to plug in the warming trays for the buns and to get the water boiling to cook the hotdogs. While she prepared lunch, Rudy grabbed another volunteer and began arranging all the gift bags in a storage room. They piled bags on gymnastic mats, on and under stacks of chairs, and in every other open area, leaving a few square feet of open floor. It worked perfectly. He'd need the remaining space later.

Rudy hadn't told the rest of the committee about Santa.

As in, he didn't have one. He had the costume, but he hadn't found a Santa-suit filler. All the actors he'd interviewed were too tall, too short, too young, or too scary. He shuddered in remembrance of the clown who'd applied for the job and had arrived in full circus regalia. That had been an immediate no.

It was on him to strap on the tummy pillow and fill the big, black boots. "Ho, ho, ho," he mumbled. He had to psych himself up in the next hour to put on a good show.

He and the rest of the committee and volunteers had arrived at nine that morning. When they opened the doors at eleven, the crowd was ready for them. A bouncing, joyous, excited group ranging from grandparents to babies in carriers. Nobody was complaining; between the anticipation of the events inside and being entertained by the reindeer outside, the wait hadn't been too onerous.

It took five minutes before he realized the Christmas carols playing through the sound system were a waste of time. The cacophony of laughter and squeals and conversation drowned out the music immediately. Rudy felt the hairs on his arms stand on end as children threw their coats at their parents and raced to whichever corner drew their attention first.

When the first kid successfully pinned the carrot on the snowman, Rudy broke into a smile so wide it hurt his face. "Mom! Mom, I won stickers!" the little girl crowed as she waved the strip of cartoon cats in her mother's face.

All the work they had put into the party was validated in a single instant.

Since everyone assumed Rudy would be organizing the Santa appearance for the final hour of the party, he hadn't been assigned any other duties. That left him free to pitch in where needed.

The games constantly had kids waiting for their turns. The crayon tables appealed to a broader age group then he expected, drawing the very little as well as the older children who were accompanying their younger siblings. He heard a few comments about not playing any baby games and waiting for Santa; he also noticed the same older kids were turning their simple pictures into multi-colour masterpieces.

When Kris waved him over, Rudy hightailed it to the serving stations. Kris handed him a hairnet and a pair of plastic gloves and set him to work stuffing buns while she prepared a fresh batch of hotdogs. "Is anyone asking for the veggie dogs?" he asked.

"We owe Cynthia a thank you for the suggestion. There won't be any left."

"We'll send her an email. How did her brother turn out as your baker's assistant?" Rudy knew from his end that Totally Iced had made their delivery date and that North Pole Unlimited expected a complete sellout.

"Pat Two did great work. So good, Aunt Vivian is looking at keeping him on as a permanent part-time staffer in the new year to help out when she returns."

A bag of hotdog buns slipped from his hands, but he caught them before they hit the floor. "Why would she need to hire someone to do that? Won't you be there?" Kris hadn't said a word about hiring her own replacement.

"I'm not certain. I was only supposed to be here

temporarily until she was back on her feet." She shrugged nonchalantly, but Rudy saw a flash of sadness on her face. "But enough about work. We're at a party," she continued. "More hotdogs!" she announced, receiving a cheer from the waiting guests.

He had set an alarm on his phone to give him a ten-minute warning to get changed for Santa's appearance. When it sounded, Kris handed off her duties to another volunteer. "What are you doing?" he asked.

"Despite our best efforts, Aunt Vivian found the elf costumes at the bottom of the pile in the storage room. I was informed it would be wasteful not to wear it while I helped Santa."

Marie had told Tucker about those costumes. "You poor thing."

She smiled, and the intensity scared him. "Thank you for your sympathy. She also sent a costume along for you. It's in the back. Come on, let's get changed."

"Um..." he stuttered as she dragged him down a corridor toward the hockey dressing rooms.

"Nope, if I can't be wasteful, neither can you."

"I, uh, already have my own costume."

Kris howled. She collapsed against a wall and doubled over; her arms wrapped around her waist. She couldn't catch her breath because she was laughing so hard, and tears streamed down her face. "Why? Why do you have your own elf costume?"

"I do not own an elf costume." That was absurd. "I rented a—" he remembered to look around to ensure there were no pint-sized eavesdroppers this time "—S-word costume. I couldn't find an actor, so I have to do it." He'd thought that was the worst thing ever to happen to him, but he was relieved to be wrong. The elf costume was scarier.

"You're going to be S-word? Why didn't you tell me?"

"I was still looking for actors until last night."

"Then you'd better hurry and get changed. We have less than ten minutes before you need to make an appearance."

She shoved him down the hall. He broke into a trot. The pillow adjustment alone would take a couple minutes. Fortunately, he could pull on the rest of his costume over his clothes.

It took quite the balancing act for him to get into the pants once he had the pillow strapped to his chest. Upon reflection, he should have put the pants and boots on first, then added the padding.

The suit itself was easy enough to don. The pants had an elastic waistband which stretched over his generous belt and had suspenders to keep them from sliding down. The large brass buttons on the coat fastened easily, and the thick black belt matched the boots. The fake-fur collar tickled his face, but once he hooked the long white beard over his ears, and added the matching wig, he didn't notice the slight scratching over the general itch attacking his face.

There wasn't a mirror, but he could see a reflection of himself in the glass front of the fire extinguisher box. He looked...passable. It was better than nothing.

"Ho, ho, ho," he said for practice before he reached for the doorknob.

Then there was nothing.

14. KRIS

KRIS SHOULD HAVE TRIED on the elf costume at home. The tiniest of the tunics hit her at the knee and the short sleeves went down to her elbows. On the other hand, the largest of the tights were too small, turning her legs into red-and-white-striped sausages. "You owe me big for this, Aunt Viv," she muttered.

She straightened the floppy hat in the mirror and adjusted the pompom. Despite the bad fit, she still thought she looked adorable. "It's only for an hour. At least I'm not dressed as Mrs. Claus." She slung a sack over each shoulder and stepped into the hall.

She reached out to knock in the storage room door to get Rudy moving, but froze when she saw him step out of the bathroom. He was a truly spectacular Kris Kringle. Bright blue eyes sparkled beneath thick white eyebrows. His face was covered with a long white beard, and an impressive moustache hid the bottom half of his nose. It looked incredibly lifelike. She'd expected cotton fluff, or a stringy nylon wig at best. "You look terrific!"

"Ho, ho, thank you, young lady." Rudy's voice was a

little lower and louder than normal, which would make it carry better in the hall over the noise from the kids. "Shall we bring out some Christmas spirit to all of these party goers?" He offered his arm.

"We shall."

The cheer was deafening. Rudy, er, Santa, swaggered to the front of the room, drawing candy canes from seemingly bottomless pockets to hand out to children along his route. Without an introduction, he began to recite "A Visit from St. Nicholas" from memory, pausing to let the kids shout out various words and phrases even the youngest of them knew, as he moved the stool they'd provided out of the way. Then he launched into a selection of "Up on the Rooftop", the first song on the singalong list. "Hello, everyone, and merry Christmas."

"Merry Christmas, Santa," they chorused back.

"There are only twenty days left until Christmas, so I'm a pretty busy fellow. Do you think my list of chores to do is this big?" He held his fingers an inch apart.

"No," shouted the crowd.

He moved his hands a foot apart. "This big?"

"No!"

He spread his arms as wide as he could. "This big?"

"Yes!"

"You're right! But I had to get away to visit all the good boys and girls and grown-ups at the North Calgary Community Christmas party. Are you having a good time? Did you all get some lunch?"

"Yes, Santa."

Kris stayed back and let Rudy work the room. He was magical. No matter where she looked, the audience was completely enthralled and engaged with the Santa at the front of the room. He led them in another song, then explained how the present delivery worked.

"Now, I'm asking you to be patient because in a few minutes, my very good friend Elf Kris is going to take charge of the presents, because I have to get back to my workshop at the North Pole."

Variations of "No, Santa, please stay" erupted from the crowd, but he raised his hands until they died down. "I'm very sorry, folks, but you saw my reindeer ride outside. We have to go. But don't worry, I'll see you again soon. But you won't see me because you'll all be asleep in your beds. Ho, ho, ho!" And then the man in red ducked out a door at the back of the room.

Kris froze. That wasn't the plan. Santa was supposed to stick around and hand out the presents himself. She had no idea what Rudy was thinking. "Fellow helpers, can you please get started on bringing out the gifts?" She raced into the corridor.

But she didn't run into Rudy. There was a door leading outside, but it was attached to the fire alarm; it would have gone off if he'd opened it to make his escape. She checked the men's bathroom, but it was empty. Then she heard pounding coming from inside the storage room.

Kris tried the handle, but it wouldn't budge. "Hello in there?"

"Kris? It's me, Rudy. I've been stuck in here forever. Get me out!"

"Why are you in the storage room?" she asked as she jiggled the handle. She jerked on it twice and heard something click inside the knob. She twisted one more time and the door flew open. She stared at Rudy in shock. "What on earth did you do to your costume?"

Gone was the spectacular Santa from minutes ago.

Rudy looked good, but second-rate to the man she'd just seen. His beard and wig were obviously fake, whereas Santa #1's could have passed as genuine. Rudy's suit hung on his padded frame; the other guy's costume was tailored to fit. It also had a different belt buckle.

"I thought I looked pretty good," Rudy said.

"You do, but why the costume change? Did you have to give the other one back by two o'clock or something? It looked really good on you. The contact lenses were amazing. How did you get them out so quickly?"

He stared at her. "What other costume? What contacts? Kris, what are you talking about? I've been stuck in that room for the last ten minutes."

"That wasn't you out there?" Her tone matched his quizzical look.

"Out where?"

"There was a Santa out there! Out there, in the hall, with us and the kids. He smiled and sang and told stories and then disappeared out the back door. I thought—we all thought—it was you!"

"It wasn't," Rudy said, crossing his heart with his fingers.

"I know that now." Her head was spinning, but she didn't have time to figure it out. "We can't let the kids see you in this Santa suit. They'll know something is wrong. Get back into the storage room. I'll bring you the other elf costume. Then you can help with the present delivery."

Rudy's face dropped, and his rosy cheeks drained of all colour. "Please, Kris, not the elf costume," he begged.

"Right now, Gillespie!" Kris was glad she kept the bag she brought for Rudy with her other belongings. She handed it through a crack in the door and headed back to the party. Then she stopped at the community centre entrance.

She had to look.

The parking lot was filled with cars except for the area near the front where the temporary reindeer paddock had been. That space was bare now, not even a whisp of straw left on the icy ground. She minced outside in her thin outfit to get a closer look. There weren't even any marks in the snow to show where the fencing had been. "Wow, they're good. And fast. How could they clean up and leave so quickly?" she whispered to herself.

"Kris!"

Jennifer beckoned from the door. She wore a gorgeous cream and red knit sweater and jeans. Kris was jealous. "The kids are two minutes from rioting."

Kris took one last look at the barren area and ran for the door. "Let's do some present-ation."

Jennifer groaned. "I've loved working with you, but I won't miss your puns."

"I don't know why. They're fun-tastic."

"Move it, elf."

The two tables they'd set up to hold gift bags were filled to overflowing by the time they returned to the front of the room. Other parent volunteers waited in the wings with more, while Jennifer took a seat, armed with a tablet and electronic pencil.

Kris clapped her hands to get everyone's attention. "Ladies and gentlemen, and especially boys and girls, we're about to get started. I know everyone is excited, but please wait until Mrs. Chang calls your name before you come to get your gift. My fellow helpers will be handing the gifts to me, and we have to make sure you and your present match before I can hand it over to you. Are you ready?"

Cheers and applause and whistles answered her. She knew Jennifer had a system, and the others were delivering the bags in a certain order. All she had to do was stand in place and call out names as the gift bags were handed to her.

It went surprisingly fast and without a hitch. Because of Jennifer's planning, they even had extra bags for four unexpected children, although those kids had to wait while the present carriers "had to dig all the way to the bottom of Santa's sack to find them."

Just as the last present was being handed out, Rudy finally reappeared. His tunic and shorts reminded her of a high school gym uniform, covering what it had to while being as unflattering as possible. The tights, which had looked mustard yellow in the bag, were a blindingly bright sunshine yellow on him. His hat was so small it sat atop his head rather than on it. He looked adorable. "Where have you been?" Kris whispered.

"I got locked in the storage room again."

15. RUDY

THE GAMES WERE PLAYED, the food was eaten, and the presents were opened. The party had been a success from start to finish. Parents hustled the last of the children back to their cars, gathering the dropped scarves and mittens the little guests left in their wakes. When only the volunteers were left, somebody turned off the carols playing in the background and silence reigned. For a moment, everyone stood still and simply enjoyed the quiet.

Rudy's first move was to get out of the elf suit. Kris changed too, although she kept the hat. Jennifer paired them together on clean-up duty, so as they filled garbage cans and recycle bins and packed boxes with leftover game pieces and prizes, they had a chance to talk.

"You must be exhausted," Rudy said.

"I am, but it's a good exhausted."

"You should be. You also finished the North Pole Unlimited contract this week. Head Office is thrilled. They expect to sell out in the preorder."

"We did make some pretty amazing cookies."

"You made me a hero for getting the contract signed, so thanks double for that."

She smiled. "You're welcome, Rudy."

"Now the party is done, too. We put a lot of work into it, and every second was worth it, but I will happily hire out the rest of my Christmas present wrapping for the rest of the year."

Kris's eyes got wide. "You aren't wrapping your own presents? Blasphemy!"

"You have a storage container full of wrapping paper and ribbons, don't you?"

She waggled two fingers.

Kris could say what she wanted about her aunt being the biggest Christmas junkie in the family, but she didn't fall far from the yule tree. "What if I stuffed them in gift bags? Would that count?"

"I suppose."

Rudy stretched, then scratched his face where the itch from the fake beard lingered. "This was a lot of fun. The kids had a blast, and I think the parents did too."

"I know they did. Your reindeer rental was inspired. Everybody loved it. I still think that was the best Santa I've ever seen." She levelled a stare at him. "Are you sure you didn't switch costumes while you were in the storage room to freak me out?"

"I'm certain. It was just me and that one awful costume."

"Then where did the other guy come from? The North Pole?"

Rudy knew it was a joke, but her crack got him thinking. He had asked everybody he knew for recommendations. Maybe one of his coworkers had arranged for a ringer.

It was a comforting idea, but he dismissed the thought as quickly as it had popped into his head. Even if someone had found a holiday Santa, they would have told him about it, if for no other reason but to avoid what did happen: having two Santas at the same location at the same time and upsetting the kids. "I have no idea."

She glared suspiciously, then burst into laughter. "If you say so."

"What will you do with all your free time now?" he asked.

"Sleep. Sleep and laundry all day tomorrow. Then I'll be relaxed and refreshed and ready to go at Totally Iced on Monday and get back to the regular Christmas madness."

That was what he hoped to hear. Despite his earlier comments, he knew neither of them were in any shape for a date the next day. "Will you be back to your regular hours?"

"Yes."

"No more working evenings, or extra early start times in the morning?"

"No, just my regular four-thirty to two-thirty."

"Will you have time later this week to go out with me? I think we deserve an extra special fancy date night. Dinner. Maybe some dancing or a show. It'll be a well-earned Christmas present to ourselves."

She nodded enthusiastically, then drew herself up short. "Are you certain you want to start something with me? I don't know how long I'll be in Calgary. I have no control over what my aunt decides. I like you a lot, and the more time we spend together, the harder it will be at the end."

"You have no idea how long you could be working

for her. And if the worst does come to pass, there are other bakeries in Calgary. They'd be lucky to have you. I think we should make the most of every day together while we have it. What do you say? Super big date night next Saturday, so you can sleep in Sunday morning?"

Kris bit her bottom lip. Then the corners of her mouth twitched.

Her answer was interrupted by a woman pushing the hall door open. "I'm sorry," Jennifer called, "the party's over. Oh, hi, Vivian."

Kris's aunt closed the door behind her. "I took an exit poll in the parking lot. This was the best party ever. I'm sorry I missed it."

Kris hurried over. "You're supposed to be home, resting."

"I'm recovering, not on my deathbed. I didn't do any of the work here, but I wanted to tell you I think you've been permanently recruited to the North Calgary Christmas Party committee. What did I hear about reindeer? People were raving."

"We had two reindeer that guests could greet as they entered the party. It was very cool," Kris said. Then she pointed at him. "It was Rudy's idea."

"It was brilliant," Vivian said to him. "Everybody loved them. A little birdie told me Cynthia Quinn bailed at the last minute and you saved the day by organizing all the games and prizes as well."

"That was Kris," Rudy said.

"Thank goodness for all those afternoons I substituted at my sister's daycare. I think the kids had fun."

"I've heard nothing but good things. You did such a good job filling in for me, I think you should be on the committee permanently. Jennifer has already asked me to convince you to come back next year."

Kris looked at Rudy, then her aunt. "I'm sure you'll be back on your feet by the time the next party rolls around," she said.

Vivian smiled at him, like she had a secret. Rudy had an idea of what was coming. "Perhaps I should excuse myself." He desperately wanted to stick around and eavesdrop, but if what he suspected was about to happened, he owed Kris her privacy.

"There is a conversation I need to have with Kris, but not here, and not now. Maybe you should come over for supper some night this week, and we can discuss whether or not you'd be interested in staying in Calgary and buying into Totally Iced. With all the new business we've picked up, I'm considering expanding. I'll need to work with someone I can trust," Vivian said to Kris. Then she added, "Does Wednesday work, or all you already engaged?" and Rudy knew why he'd been invited to hang around.

"We don't have anything planned for Wednesday. She'd be delighted to have dinner with you," he answered on her behalf.

"Excellent. I need to talk to Jennifer for a moment. I'll be right back."

He waited till Vivian was out of earshot before he nudged Kris. "Breathe."

"Did you hear that?"

"I was standing right here."

"She wants me to stay. As a partner, Rudy!"

"I know."

"I don't know what to say. I'd hoped she'd ask me to keep working for her, but I never dreamed of becoming a partner in the business. It would be my own bakery. Partly my own bakery. It's everything I've been working toward." She could hardly speak as she shook with excitement. Her grin was contagious.

"It is. Why don't you know what to say? Are you having second thoughts about staying in town?" He thought she'd seize the opportunity without hesitation. He wanted her to.

"No, not at all." Kris blew out a breath. "This is life-changing news. I want to be able to tell her I considered every angle with a clear head, and my head is whirling right now."

The stars in her eyes warmed his heart. There was no question; she wanted this. It would be terrific for her career, and fantastic for their burgeoning relationship. "Can I encourage you for mostly selfish reasons, or do you want me to offer silent support while you make your decision?" He could keep his hopeful comments to himself... for a while.

"You can be selfish. Some of my reasons to say yes are."

Rudy looked around the hall. Vivian was busy speaking with Jennifer, and the other volunteers were still engaged in cleaning. He leaned forward. "How's this for an argument," he whispered, then leaned in even further until his lips brushed hers.

"Ho, ho, ho!" called another woman who burst into the hall.

"Are you kidding me?" he muttered at the latest interruption.

Kris snickered.

"Is there a Vivian or Kris Singleton here?" the woman called as she scanned the room. When she finished unwinding the scarf from around her neck and removed her toque, Rudy looked twice at her face. He was certain he knew her, but he couldn't place her. The short brown hair, the laughing brown eyes, the bubbly voice.

Wait a minute. He recognized that voice.

"Hey, look, it's the miracle worker and the miracle baker! Just the people I was looking for," she said.

He almost had it. Then she kept talking. "Nick put a cap on the number of units North Pole Unlimited staff could order from the Twelve Sales of Christmas, so I convinced him I needed to do an HR surprise inspection on all our western Canada sites. I left my last batch of paperwork with Tucker at the office, which means I have an entire suitcase I can fill with chocolate meringues while I'm in Calgary. It would be wasteful to take it home empty."

"Jilly Lewis?" he said slowly.

She waved. "Hi, Rudy. Great job on getting Totally Iced on board. Nice to meet you, Miss Singleton. Can I call you Kris? I'm such a fan of your bakery that I feel like we're already friends."

"Of course. I've heard all about you and your admiration for our cookies," Kris said.

"Let's be honest, it's an obsession. I'm not ashamed of it. I'm slightly ashamed of buying out your store this afternoon, but the lady behind the counter said you'd be glad to see them gone and you were planning to restock with new cookie varieties on Monday anyway."

Rudy was still suck on the fact Jilly Lewis was in Calgary. "What are you doing here?"

"I told you. I'm doing spot checks on all our businesses to ensure proper human resources policies are being followed and enforced."

He'd heard stories of Jilly. Of her off-the-wall requests and the resulting chaos. Wherever she stuck her nose, weirdness followed. "That's all?"

"What else could it be? Besides the cookies, but I already copped to those." She spun around, taking in the nearly cleaned room. "Tucker said you were one of the hosts of the community Christmas party. It looks like I missed it. How did it go?"

"Fine," he said.

Vivian and Jennifer joined the group, and he made the necessary introductions. Jennifer Chang was particularly happy to shake Jilly's hand. "I can't tell you how much we appreciated all of North Pole Unlimited's corporate donations. The gift bags, the candy canes, the luncheon supplies, the cash for the presents. It wouldn't have been nearly the success it was if it wasn't for you."

Jilly accepted the praise gracefully. "We're always happy to support community-building events."

Kris raised her hand. "Wait a minute! The luncheon supplies? As in the plates, the napkins, the cutlery?"

"Exactly."

"They came from North Pole Unlimited?"

Jilly and Jennifer shared a confused look. "One of our suppliers, yes. Why?" Jilly asked.

Kris covered her face and stifled a groan. "Do you know how much time I spent trying to return that box? Everybody insisted they had the right shipping address, but I knew I hadn't ordered any of it."

Jennifer slowly raised her hand. "I always have that stuff shipped to the bakery. Vivian stores it for us. I guess I forgot to tell you."

Kris whirled on her aunt. "Why didn't you say anything?"

"You didn't tell me you were getting shipments. If you'd mentioned it, I would have set you straight."

When she bowed her head again, Rudy pulled her into a sympathetic hug. "You'll know for next year."

She stilled in his arms, then stared at the trio that had caused her so much grief. "What about the costumes?"

Vivian smirked. "You were working so hard, I thought you deserved a laugh. I didn't think you'd actually wear them."

"You. Coal. Stocking," Kris threatened, eliciting laughs from everybody else.

"Help me out here, Rudy," Vivian begged.

"Are you kidding? There was an elf costume in that box for me too."

"Please?"

"I'll think about it. What about hiring St. Nick?" Rudy asked.

His question was met with silence.

"What about St. Nick?" Jennifer asked.

"Come on, you can admit it now. Who did it and where did you find him? I called everyone who owed me a favour, and nothing. I want to say thank you."

"What are you talking about? You were Santa. I reimbursed you for the suit rental, which was a steal for the quality. You looked great," Jennifer said.

Kris came to his defense. "It wasn't him. Remember when Santa ducked out the back before we handed out the gifts, and I ran to bring him back? I found Rudy locked in a storage closet, wearing an obviously rented suit. He says he was there the whole time, and he had no idea there was another Santa in the building."

"He was Rudy's height and shape, except for the padded belly. They even had the same voice. If it wasn't

Rudy, who was it?" Jennifer looked at Vivian expectantly, who shrugged.

"What about you, Jilly? It's awfully convenient you appear on the same day as a mystery Santa when North Pole Unlimited is one of the primary sponsors of the Christmas party. You knew I've asked everyone in the company if they could recommend a St. Nicholas. Are you sure you didn't pack an extra holiday surprise in your suitcase?"

"Don't be silly. How could I have possibly packed a six-foot tall, blue eyed, white-haired, white-bearded mystery man in my suitcase?"

Rudy levelled his brown eyes on her. "How did you know he had blue eyes?"

Jilly pulled her phone from her pocket and pressed a button. It beeped at her. "Wow. Would you look at the time? I must be off!" She hugged Vivian and thanked her again for supplying her with cookies for the season. When Jennifer shook her hand, Jilly promised to be in touch for next year's party. Then she came over to him and Kris.

"I've heard nothing but good things about you two from Jennifer. I'm very pleased we had a small hand in what sounds like such an important event in your community. Congratulations on a fantastic party, and thanks for all your hard work."

Kris shook her hand heartily. "Thanks for pushing for the chocolate meringue contract. I'm glad we decided to do it, and if we have any more customers as grateful as you, it will be totally worth it."

"I'll recruit more myself. Payment to be made in other baked goods."

"It's a deal," Kris replied with a laugh.

Then Jilly turned to him. "You didn't do bad either, St. Nick."

"The other Santa was your doing, right?"

"Wow, my Uber to the airport is here already." Jilly pulled her white, red, and grey sock-monkey toque over her head. "Merry Christmas to all, and to all a good afternoon."

"She's a real holiday whirlwind," Vivian commented.

"That was five minutes. Can you imagine working with her regularly?" Rudy asked.

"Not without getting a headache," Kris said with a laugh.

It didn't take long to load the vehicles, take out the trash, and lock the doors to the community centre. The room would soon be used by another group for another purpose, but Rudy had the feeling the good vibes from the party would linger a while.

He and Kris paused between their vehicles. "Now that you plan to stay in Calgary, can we start filling our calendars with dates?" There was so much he could show her about her new hometown. They'd need days to discover all the hidden gems of the city, months to explore the surrounding area. Even that might not be long enough.

"I haven't said I'm staying for sure."

"You're going to tell your aunt no?"

She laughed. "Of course not, but sometimes a girl needs to play a little hard to get to feel appreciated."

"Will you play hard to get if I asked you to join my dodgeball team for the session starting in February?"

"No. It'll be fun to play together again."

"Would it be hard to convince you to go to the Arrowhead concert in January?"

"Not in the slightest."

"What if I asked you to be my date to a New Year's Eve party?"

"I'd say yes."

"Yeah, you're playing really hard to get, Singleton."

Kris leaned forward and rose to her toes to give him a smack right on the lips. "I'm not hard for *you* to get, Gillespie. Just Aunt Vivian. She needs some payback for the costumes."

Rudy pulled her in for a much deeper, longer kiss. He wasn't even pretending he was hard to get when it came to Kris. She already had him. Her aunt deserved some payback but, "On the other hand, she is the reason you were on the party committee and we spent time together and you finally went out with me, so maybe you should cut her a little slack."

"If you give me another kiss, I'll think about it."

Rudy thought about those elf tights. And then about the woman in his arms. And then he kissed her again.

EPILOGUE

NORTH POLE UNLIMITED HEADQUARTERS,
December, Manitoba

"This is quite the spread, Jilly." Nick Klassen looked at the pair of dainty trays on the sideboard in the meeting room. They were loaded with delicious confections: iced cookies covered in sprinkles, bars drizzled with chocolate, unadorned shortbread dotted with chopped cranberries and curls of orange zest. He was tempted to skip the soup and sandwiches they'd ordered in from Norma's Buns and dive right into dessert.

"It's the second last staff meeting before Christmas. I finished the western Canada human resources report, and the Twelve Sales of Christmas promotion was a huge success. We've all earned a treat." His assistant snagged a shortbread cookie and popped it into her mouth. "These are so good."

"I'm not seeing any chocolate meringues on these trays."

"I barely share those with Dan, and I gave birth to him. I'm not putting them out for the masses. If you wanted some, you should have ordered your two-and-only-two-per-employee boxes."

Yeah, he'd be paying for that rule for a while. "You tried to order ten boxes, and bribed Joy McCall to order another ten for you!"

"And if I had all those cookies, I would have given you some. So, really, it's your own fault you don't have any delicious chocolate meringues."

"You could still share. I know you got some in Calgary."

"Prove it, boss," she dared.

The boardroom got louder as a handful of department heads entered and circled the table, choosing their lunches while they still had options. Hollis Dash was in town and arrived with a tablet in each hand; it was better than the time he'd brought six three-ring binders full of contract copies and notes. Nick knew Dr. Farnsworth was out sick, which meant Joy would be sitting in for her boss to give the Animal Care department report, which meant she and Decker would be giving each other not-so-furtive glances all through lunch. He understood. If his fiancée worked at North Pole Unlimited, he'd sit beside her at management meetings too.

Seeing all the pairings gave him an idea. "Maybe you're saving those chocolate meringues for somebody special. Somebody who might be arriving in December in a couple hours and is known to enjoy cookies with his evening hot chocolate at the Pumpkin Patch, but whose rig has been seen parked outside a private residence the last couple times he's been in town," Nick hinted.

"If you stop, I'll give you two."

He quirked an eyebrow at her.

"Three, but no more. Not even Dan gets more than that."

"Three," he agreed, astounded Jilly had caved so easily.

Payback was going to be fun.

***

THE END

RECIPE - CHOCOLATE CHIP CHERRY COCONUT COOKIES

(MAKES 2 dozen)

1/3 cup – 75 mL margarine/butter
1/2 cup – 125 mL granulated sugar
1 egg
1/2 tsp – 2 mL almond extract (can substitute vanilla)
3/4 cup – 175 mL all-purpose flour
1/2 tsp – 2 mL baking powder
3/4 cup – 175 mL semi-sweet chocolate chips (can substitute white chocolate chips)
1/2 cup – 125 mL shredded coconut
1/2 cup – 125 mL chopped maraschino cherries (red or green or both if you want to be really festive)

Preheat oven to 325F / 160C.

. . .

Cream butter and sugar. Beat in egg, extract flour and baking powder. Add remaining ingredients and mix well. Drop by spoonful onto a greased cookie sheet and bake for 15-17 minutes. Transfer to wire racks to cool.

These cookies stay soft in an airtight container.

Fall a Million Times

A Million Love Notes

ROYAL OAK RANCH

The Cowboy and the Movie Star

The Cowboy and the Pastry Princess

The Cowboy and the Constable

RESORT ROMANCES

Cuban Moon

Mexican Sunsets

Dominican Stars

Mayan Midnights

Complete 4 book boxed set

HEARTMADE COLLECTION

Brunch

Mains & Sides

Holiday Table

ABOUT THE AUTHOR

Elle Rush is a sweet contemporary romance author from Winnipeg, Manitoba, Canada. When she's not travelling, she's hard at work writing books which are set all over the world. From Hollywood to the house next door, her heroes will make you sigh, and her heroines will make you laugh out loud.

Elle has a degree in Spanish and French, barely passed German, and is learning Italian. She flunked poetry in every language she ever studied. She also has mild addictions to tea, yarn, terrible sci-fi movies, and home renovation shows.

To keep up with news and upcoming releases, sign up for her newsletter at **www.ellerush.com/news-letter**, or follow her on Twitter (@elle_rush) or Facebook (Elle.Rush.Romance).

www.ingramcontent.com/pod-product-compliance
Lightning Source LLC
Chambersburg PA
CBHW051943220626
47052CB00004B/780